"*Hunger* is a masterwork of enormous power. This is a collection I return to for its beauty, love, and grace. I carry Lan Samantha Chang's vivid characters in my heart."

—Min Jin Lee, author of
Free Food for Millionaires and *Pachinko*

"One day, decades ago, I picked up *Hunger*, and found I could not put it down. In a way, I've never stopped reading the book: I teach the stories to my students; I study the way the sentences fix themselves into crystalline prose; I invite in all the ghosts. Lan Samantha Chang has not only influenced my own development as a writer, she's one of the most influential writers in American letters full stop. *Hunger* is a masterpiece, a necessary haunting."

—Justin Torres, author of *We the Animals*

"This remarkable first book has a deeply tragic sensibility, but it whispers its tragedy, thereby heightening it. *Hunger* evinces in many ways the quintessential voice of the immigrant, obscured by longings, distance and nostalgia, muted by language itself, yet resolutely insistent: These stories . . . will not be silenced."   —*Portland Oregonian*

"In clear, often shining prose she paints the world of Asian-American immigrants. . . . *Hunger* places Chang firmly among the group of novelists whose writing about lost homelands has received high acclaim: Oscar Hijeulos, Christina Garcia, Amy Tan, Edwige Danticat, Julia Alvarez, and Junot Diaz."   —*Milwaukee Journal Sentinel*

"These radiant, heartbreaking, soul-touching tales form a working definition of all we hunger for. Lan Samantha

Chang writes beautifully of the hungers of the heart: of desire, of ambition; of all we might be, and aren't; of all we most want, and can't have."

—Andrea Barrett, author of *Natural History*

"Lan Samantha Chang writes superbly about the intricacies of exile and especially about women in exile, caught between the present and the past, their husbands and their children. *Hunger* is a wonderfully accomplished first collection from a writer whose work we will be reading for many years to come."

—Margot Livesey, author of *The Boy in the Field*

"That Chang is able to evoke so nuanced a reaction is a testament to her unrelenting dramatic vision, her depth and subtlety of insight and her beautiful, merciless prose."

—*Boston Book Review*

"Poignant. . . . Chang is able to sketch quickly complex personalities caught in a ghetto-like emotional condition. [Her] descriptions recall Henry Roth's or Bernard Malamud's immigrant families of the turn of the century."

—*Philadelphia Inquirer*

"Chang's clear, crisp prose makes the everyday world of Chinese immigrants depicted in her short stories and novella one of great intensity."   —*Harvard Book Review*

"A wonderfully written debut collection. . . . [W]ith considerable insight and originality. . . . [A] somber, vivid, deeply original vision of Asian-American life. . . . The debut of a writer possessing a distinctive, fresh imagination and voice."   —*Kirkus Reviews*

HUNGER

Also by Lan Samantha Chang

THE FAMILY CHAO

ALL IS FORGOTTEN, NOTHING IS LOST

INHERITANCE

HUNGER

A Novella and Stories

LAN
SAMANTHA
CHANG

Foreword by Alexander Chee

W. W. NORTON & COMPANY
Celebrating a Century of Independent Publishing

Portions of this book have appeared, in slightly different form, in *The Atlantic Monthly, Story, New Letters, Prairie Schooner, The Best American Short Stories 1994,* and *The Best American Short Stories 1996.*

For information about permission to reproduce selections from this book, write to Permissions, W. W. Norton & Company, Inc., 500 Fifth Avenue, New York, NY 10110.

For information about special discounts for bulk purchases, please contact W. W. Norton Special Sales at specialsales@wwnorton.com or 800-233-4830

Manufacturing by Lakeside Book Company
Book design by Judith Stagnitto Abbate
Production manager: Devon Zahn

ISBN 978-1-324-06456-5 pbk.

W. W. Norton & Company, Inc.
500 Fifth Avenue, New York, N.Y. 10110
www.wwnorton.com

W. W. Norton & Company Ltd.
15 Carlisle Street, London W1D 3Bs

1 2 3 4 5 6 7 8 9 0

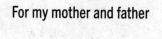

For my mother and father

CONTENTS

FOREWORD

IN AN INTERVIEW SHE GAVE TO THE *MORNING News* in 2005 Lan Samantha Chang described herself as someone who had at first wanted to write novels, many novels, but could not write stories more than twenty-five pages long. And the stories do have a remarkable, almost paradoxical density to them, a weight that also seems carried so easily on her sentences.

She told the interviewer David Birnbaum that she was trying to break it to her family that she would be an artist, aiming for a rebellion and acknowledging that it looked at first like she'd acquiesced to their plans for her by attending Yale, Harvard, Iowa, and Stanford. By the time she got to Iowa she was writing. Her parents thought of her as sowing wild oats, as if she were a bachelor putting off getting married. One of her sisters told people she was going to journalism school. "I am working up to the big rebellion," she said. And it may be that writing the rebellious daughter characters in her debut collection was like a rehearsal for doing the same herself. But it may be she had her eye on something else.

CHANG was thirty-one years old in 1998 when she made her debut with *Hunger*. The reviews were raves, the praise incandescent. The *New York Times* profiled her two years after publication as if to observe just how extraordinary the collection and the reviews had been. The critics said often that Chang was writing about lost homelands but you will see that these are stories mostly about the new homeland, not lost at all. These are mostly stories about America, about people who gave up everything to move here only to learn they would need to give up even more. People who fled China for Taiwan and who then had to flee Taiwan as well.

"Pipa's Story," set firmly in China, is the last story in the collection and the first story she published. It appeared in the *Atlantic* in 1993 and was selected for *Best American Short Stories 1994*, edited by Tobias Wolff. The attention she received after that story alone nearly got her a book deal but she wanted to choose her moment. "I was afraid of being that young writer whose acclaim surprised me into silence. I wanted to wait until I knew what and who I wanted to be as a writer," she said. After she appeared in *Best American Short Stories 1996*, edited by John Edgar Wideman, with "The Eve of the Spirit Festival," published in *Prairie Schooner* in 1995, she seemed to know something more of what and who she wanted to be, and this is the result.

Hunger takes its name from a novella Chang said she wrote in six months, a short time by her measure. *Hunger* is a tour de force, told from the point of view of a mother describing the war that develops between her demanding, disappointed husband, Tian, and his demanding, disappointed daughter Ruth. Their inability to see how alike they are, to apologize to each other, each brings the other to their knees, a final, doubled humiliation that overshadows the mother and the other sister. But this is no ordinary story of tragedy, and in the determination of the mother, speaking from beyond the grave, to tell the story of her husband, her daughters, and herself, we find a very different kind of beauty, love, and intelligence. I won't ever forget Tian, who carried his violin wrapped in oil cloth over his head as he swam to the boat that helped him escape China and then had to spend his life as an adjunct at a music school that would not give him tenure but tried to take credit for the education he gave his daughter.

While her stories here do have some themes that repeat, they each feel distinct. It is not repeating oneself when writing about Chinese immigrants in the mid- to late-twentieth century who have highly educated professional fathers working in restaurants, fathers who are passed over for promotions, fathers with defiant daughters. There are also the mothers who feel trapped by their husbands' decisions or their husbands' failures, the mothers who feel betrayed by their daughters' independence and even their childhood rebellions. But the stories do not blend together.

Reading this collection now it feels like the kind of story collection you could educate yourself with — on how to treat your parents, your spouse, your children — in order to avoid the conflicts here. It is a wise book, for the way it is full of the sorts of mistakes people make and cannot take back. But what's more, the haunting decision in one story to skip drinks with coworkers contrasts with the haunting decision to host drinks for coworkers too many times in another. You as the reader come to understand the way it doesn't matter. There is no special key here at least to get your coworkers to understand that you're human, that you fear you could die in front of them and it wouldn't matter. I see the stories as being about people lost inside of a system indifferent to their survival, and indifferent to the beliefs they have about what it takes to succeed.

There are no weak stories in this collection. And if Chang seems to know a great deal about the violin in these stories, or the life of the precocious performer, she was a precocious violinist as a child. If she seems to know the Midwest, she was born in Appleton, Wisconsin, in 1965. Her parents are Chinese immigrants who came to the United States in the 1950s—a chemical engineer and a piano teacher. There is something especially moving about the way they helped her with the research she did at Princeton for her first novel, *Inheritance*, helping her with the Chinese translations of the materials.

She has published only novels since this first collection, three of them, no other stories thus far. The titular novella, *Hunger*, in that context, would seem to be where she broke free from who she had been, the writing of it letting her reach for who she would eventually become.

FULL disclosure: I was a classmate of Chang's at the Iowa Writers' Workshop, a year behind her. She had the blithe confidence of a house captain when she hosted us for supper, and she still does in her role as director, a job she took back in 2005, where I also taught alongside her in 2011 when I was invited there.

In preparing to write this, I found myself reading the profiles, the interviews, seeing how the young writer declared she would do X, and the next iteration of her declared it done, whether it was writing a novel when she was ready to do so or raising funds from donors to give the writers at the Workshop more support. She has attained enough to receive the sort of introduction I hate: "I don't need to list all of her many fellowships and awards," this kind of introduction begins, and yet you do, you should: she had to earn them to be where she is, writing as she is, in America.

This book returns now to a publishing landscape that is very different from the one in which it first was published. Imagine back to when the many successful writers of color Chang has shepherded just through the Iowa Writers' Workshop in her time as the director have not even imagined themselves as writers yet. Some are yet to be born. There were so few Asian American women writers that Chang was compared to two writers she does not at all resemble in style—Amy Tan and Maxine Hong Kingston—and who are in turn very different from each other. Whatever big rebellion she had on her mind back in 2005, she is one of the few American writers who can be said to have actively worked to change the literary landscape in which she is understood, helping to create a more diverse literature in which she might actually be seen for the writer she is.

Please welcome again Lan Samantha Chang and *Hunger*.

ALEXANDER CHEE
2023

HUNGER

HUNGER

I OFTEN DREAM ABOUT THE RESTAU-
RANT where I met Tian. Late at night, in these blue rooms,
the memory flickers up before me, dim and silent, never
changing. I see the simple neon sign that reads "Vermilion
Palace." The drifting snow blows up against the scarlet
double doors. I see myself walking toward those doors—a
slight, brown girl with hair like an inkbrush, tilted eyes,
and a wary mouth.

For my first few months in New York City, I could
not stay warm. I wore a heavy coat and wound myself in
woolen scarves, but the chill went deep beneath my skin,
and the winter wind found every crevice as I walked to
the restaurant on numb feet, past the subway stop, the
university, and the music school, my gaze fixed on the icy
pavement to keep myself from falling. I could not taste my
food or feel the softness of my narrow bed. I had been in
the city for two months before I even noticed the music
school. And then one evening I heard a student practicing.
Walking past a basement window, I caught the thread of

a violin melody, high and sweet as a woman's voice. The sound rose up through a crack in the window and between the safety bars; it shimmered through me, a wave of color, blooming past the gray tenements and toward the narrow sky. I drew one cold, sweet breath of air and truly understood that I had arrived in America.

A few days later, I saw Tian. He might have been to the restaurant a dozen times before, but I do not remember seeing him until after the music. I noticed him on a stormy evening near the end of winter. He arrived just at the time of day when the low, gray light changes to dusk. I was standing at the window, watching the falling snow make bright flecks in the headlamps of the taxicabs, when a man appeared in the doorway, carrying a violin case.

"One person," he said, in confident English. At that time, in 1967, many new Chinese had come to live on Manhattan's Upper West Side. Most of them turned up at the restaurant, sooner or later. But not many spoke English with such ease. He wore a brown felt hat, and his overcoat seemed cut to fit his shoulders; most of the other men seemed content to wear whatever would make do.

"Come with me," I replied, in Mandarin. I did not want him to hear my voice in broken English words.

I seated him and poured his tea, looking down at the swirl of leaves in the water. I felt the heat of the steam in my face, the warm steel handle in my hands; I watched the tea leaves drift and slide against the blue and white cup. He thanked me in Chinese. His dark eyes followed the line of my face, my throat, down to my starched white shirt. For the first time, I felt warm.

Before I left Taiwan, my mother had said, "Beware abnormally pale men. Beware a man whose cheekbones are too high or low. Watch out for one who smiles too much. And stay away from a man who gambles." Her warnings implied that I had a choice; that these things lay under my control. But when I was a child she had often talked about the Chinese myth that every man and every woman was joined at birth to their mate by an invisible, enchanted thread. With this story, she said that there could be no controlling fate.

The strange man ordered beef noodle soup and drank it quickly. He had placed his violin case in the opposite chair, upright and facing him like a lover. I watched his ivory chopsticks flash, and I envied the violin case, dark and slender, curved like a woman. Then he glanced at his watch. He flung down a dollar, seized his coat and violin, and walked out the door. I looked twice to make sure it was true: he had forgotten his hat on the chair.

To this day I don't know why I stole Tian's hat. Perhaps his solitude gave me strength. I looked around to make sure no one watched me. Then I slipped over to his table and picked up the hat, brought it back behind my counter. He had printed his name inside: Tian Sung.

I waited through my shift. Da Dao, the manager, left to fix a leak in the kitchen, so I stood at the window, idle, as the wind blew mittens and lost bus passes past my eyes. The traffic thinned out, and a red-striped awning tumbled down the avenue. Toward the end of my shift, I caught Da Dao in the storeroom sipping from a flask. He offered to snap a week of beans in exchange for my silence, but I promised I wouldn't tell anyone.

Late that night, when the busboys had begun to vacuum under the chairs, the man reappeared in the doorway. I still remember his bare, wet head and sodden trench coat, creased with snow. He walked over and stood before me.

"You might have something of mine," he said, in Mandarin this time.

"I don't think so."

"Would you please take a look?"

I bent and looked under the counter. There was the hat, where I had hidden it, on the shelf behind some extra bud vases. I knelt and took it into my hands.

Seconds passed. "Did you find a hat?" I heard him ask. I stood up and nodded, then shook my head.

"Are you all right?"

I held my hands behind the counter and did not answer.

I could not give him the hat. My hands grew cold; I could not breathe. I looked at him. The storm had streaked his hair into his eyes—surely the blackest eyes of any man I'd ever met, the eyelashes laid flat with melting snow. They held an expression of deep and painful privacy. And at that moment I believed I knew what would come to be. When I returned the hat, I would exchange it for the man who wore it. My senses opened; I grew large. I believed I heard, in the howling wind, a voice of admonition, but in the end I listened to the plunge and whistle of my blood. I put the hat into his beautiful, long-fingered hands.

BEHIND this painted wall, beneath this layer of new sheathing, hides the story of our lives together. I have been silent many years, and my daughters have chosen to forget, but our family story lingers here. It waits under the floor; it has slid into the crawl space, wound around the stubborn beams and girders that were already old thirty years ago, when Tian and I first came to live in Brooklyn.

At that time, the brownstones had begun to wear away. They stood in patient rows, like tablets in a sol-diers' graveyard, crumbled and soft around the edges. We considered other places: a Chinatown walk-up owned by Dao, a drafty room near the music school, and even a little

Midtown flat, as clean and perfect as a jewel box; but we decided to live here. It seemed that nothing in the world could disturb us on this neglected street, in these softly falling houses.

Our third-floor flat, the "servants' quarters," pleased me with its wide back windows, sloping floors, and odd-shaped rooms that had been planned and built according to someone's idea of what servants might want or need. The spacious kitchen and living room invited company, togetherness, and warmth.

The two small bedrooms stared from opposite ends of the flat. In the back bedroom, off the kitchen, I planned a nursery for the son I hoped to bear. I loved to stand in that room and look out of its one large window, past the iron fire stairs and over the small backyards, crisscrossed by a lattice of laundry lines. I saw rows of neat, gray rooftops, treetops, electricity lines, and, far away, depending on the weather, the gray or glittering cutout of Manhattan. And it seemed to me that all the safety in the world had been tucked into this space, that my children would look out at the world and know that all was well.

Tian focused his desires on a different part of the house. Behind the foyer stood a spacious walk-in closet that had been refitted as a greenhouse, with a skylight and glass shelves. This would be his music room. He removed the shelves, soundproofed the walls with pressed Styrofoam, and repainted them eggshell white. He found an old upright piano at a junk shop on Coney Island Beach and convinced someone at the restaurant to help him move it up the stairs. Finally, he produced from his briefcase a metal music stand, which unfolded at the top into fragile, steel wings.

"Now I can work and be near you." He reached to touch my face. I stood perfectly still, arrested by the scent of his hand. Desire soaked through my skin—this warmth, which had first blossomed while I poured his tea and now flowed through me at his touch. In those early days, the feeling would come over me even when I was alone, looking out the window, or standing behind the counter at the restaurant. My breath would stop in my throat, my skin would flush, and I would feel the warmth steeping through my blouse until I had to step out for fresh air or run to the bathroom to wash my face.

We made love on the floor of the new practice room. I remember my belief—a moment of certainty just prior to abandoning thought—that our moans and cries and our foreign words of love would permeate the walls of the apartment and transform the place.

Later, after I had gone to sleep, the telephone rang: it was my mother calling from Taiwan. I sat on the bed in the dark with the phone in my hand, looking out the window, where light from the streetlamp streamed over the cracked sidewalk like frost.

"I have been thinking of you," my mother said. "I have been thinking about you all day."

She had a way of guessing what I wanted. This ability, which had been so comforting to us both when I was young, had grown more difficult as I had gotten older, and after the death of my father it had become unbearable for both of us. For this reason, among others, we agreed I should go to the United States. My mother wrote a letter to a man who had owed my father a favor, asking him to claim me as a paper relative.

"I'm fine," I said. "There's nothing new."

"How is your English class?" I had stopped attending months before.

"It's fine."

"You need to learn English," she told me.

"I know a lot of it," I said.

"You aren't studying," my mother said. "Instead, you have met a man and married."

"That is not how or why it happened."

"Where is he now?"

"He is in the music room, practicing."

I listened to the thrum of the lines between us. Far away, I could hear the faint thread of the violin. Had I said something wrong? I took a breath and waited for sharp words. But she said simply, "It is *yuanfen*." For as long as I remembered, she used this expression only when discussing marriage, but she never would explain.

"What do you mean by *yuanfen*?"

She thought for a minute and replied, "It means: that apportionment of love which is destined for you in this world."

TIAN'S connection to the music school was, in his view, tenuous. After completing a master's degree, he had been kept on as an instructor of pre-college students, a position that gave him, and several others, an opportunity to display their teaching and performing skills in pursuit of an assistant professorship. He planned to give his junior-faculty recital in March. That winter, after we moved to Brooklyn, he shut himself in the tiny room for hours every day. He always kept the door closed—he had reached a point with these recital pieces where the smallest issues were significant and demanded his private concentration. From the kitchen, I listened to his faint practicing; the soundproofing did not completely block the music but blurred and softened it, absorbing it deep within the wall.

On the morning of Tian's recital, I woke up alone. As I lay in bed, listening to his swooping, dizzying warm-up scales, I suddenly felt our narrow room pitch up and down like a ship on a swell. I tumbled out of bed and staggered to the bathroom, where I bent down and seized the toilet, waiting there until I was sick. As I knelt against the cold floor and vomited again, I understood that Tian and I would have a child. It seemed to me that some spiritual power had focused upon me—that I knelt before a tablet of our ancestors. I wanted to meditate, burn incense as a sign of thanks to them and as a caution against any harm that might come, and my heart filled with a powerful gratitude and relief.

A moment later I found myself in the hallway, breathing hard, my hand on the knob of the door to Tian's little room. The music stopped. Cautiously I turned the knob. But he had not heard; he re-tuned his instrument and impatiently began his piece again. Perhaps it would not be wise to share my news, so close to his recital. After all, we had not planned for this. I tiptoed away.

That evening we had a light dinner and left early. We boarded the subway, sitting side by side as if we were brother and sister. I stretched my legs in front of me to make him notice my new shoes. But he did not notice. I stared at the soft, black shoes myself as we lurched along in the empty car.

The steel car roared and rushed. We held Tian's violin case over our laps; he clutched the canvas cover tightly. The fluorescent lights cast bruised shadows on his high, sallow cheekbones and lavender mouth. I would have tried to reassure him, but I felt as if I were encased in a bubble of happiness and illness. I did not want to ruin his concentration. I folded my gloved, trembling hands over the violin case; I had dressed protectively in a hat, a scarf, and a long wool coat.

We arrived early, to an almost empty recital hall. Far to the left, by himself, sat an older man with a thick head of gray hair and a big mustache. This, Tian whispered, was Professor Spaeth, his former teacher and now his dean. Every now and then, someone would come up and chat with Spaeth for a minute or two, but his responses were brief, and none of the visitors stayed for long.

Tian vanished into a door next to the stage. I sat alone in the third row, too shy to turn around and watch the students and colleagues who came in groups of twos or threes and scattered themselves among the seats. They spoke fluently, as carelessly as the American customers in the restaurant. I listened to their English and knew that I would not be able to hold my own in any conversation. I could only make out a few words, including "teacher," "China," "curious."

Before I came to this country, I felt at home in the Chinese language, the way a fish feels at home in the sea. When I came to New York I vowed to practice speaking English, but it was difficult, working in the restaurant. I did not talk to customers; I did not own a television. I took classes at a community college but made little progress with the humped and tangled grammar. Instead, I spent my spare time reading novels I bought and traded with the other waitresses, books that had seduced me with their bright, familiar covers, lined up along the shelves in the Chinatown stores.

Now, as I sat alone, I was overtaken by fear. I longed to be back home in Brooklyn, curled up in Tian's big chair, with a Chinese storybook in my hand. The lights dimmed and Tian took the stage with John O'Neill, his accompanist and officemate. I had never met John, although Tian often spoke about him, and I was surprised by his height, his reddish beard. The audience gave a generous welcome. The clapping died down, the two men bowed, then took their places, Tian in front of the piano.

His bow struck the strings. It seemed to drop from

above, the way a hawk will plunge with sudden swiftness to its victim. Tian bent and swayed in the vivid light, dark and wild and foreign, altogether unfamiliar. A vein in his right jaw, which I had only briefly noticed, rippled and stood out. It was like watching a man have a seizure. He terrified me. His music shuddered through me with a violence I am not sure I can describe—now delicate and now enormous, but always more powerful than his swaying, fragile figure on the stage. I felt as if he had achieved these sounds through a feat of magic or theft. I found myself pulling away from him, my back pressed tight against the chair.

How could I have chosen such an unforgiving man? I knew nothing about music, but I could hear in these sounds a man who would accept no excuse from anyone or anything close to him. The violin, uncaged from the practice room, filled the recital hall with a clear intensity; each note attacked the air, quick and piercing as a dagger. I fought an urge to run from the auditorium. Finally, he stopped. There came a prolonged and steady storm of applause. I kept my wet hands tightly folded. Tian looked straight at me and smiled, reappearing from this monstrousness. Then I did applaud. He raised the violin and began his next piece.

Afterwards, we stood next to a bowl of orange punch. Tian spoke to the people who crowded us. Sometimes he made an introduction: "Min, this is Jennings. He and I share a practice locker." I nodded and smiled. "He did fine job! He very good!" they assured me, so I nodded and smiled again. Sometimes I turned to Tian for a translation, but he seemed to be having problems with his English; he stumbled over certain words and leaned toward the others as if he couldn't hear what they were saying.

He wouldn't move from my side, and he clutched his violin case in his hand. I noticed it needed a new cover and the leather straps on the handle looked worn. I frowned;

it seemed wrong that his colleagues should see him with such old things. His black wingtips were brightly polished but rounded at the soles and heels. The lapels of his jacket had frayed a little. Since our marriage, I had watched over his eating and sleeping habits, but I needed to spend more time mending his clothes and coaxing him to buy new things. I felt relieved that his overcoat hung around the corner, on the coatrack, where no one would see how shabby it was.

Tian's colleagues lingered on, congratulating him. They fixed upon him with alert attention, as if he had sprung up, suddenly, into the light. This puzzled me, since I had seen them before while visiting the school and they had paid Tian little notice.

I remember one woman in particular, redheaded and milky-pale. This was Lydia Borgmann, whom Tian had told me about: an instructor in the same year as Tian, one of his colleagues who was vying for a professorship. She was only about my size, but she wore stacked heels that brought her closer in height to the others. She kept putting her hand on Tian's arm—not necessarily to flirt, I decided after watching her closely, but to give an impression of friendship. Tian felt so happy about the recital he did not even notice. He bent his head in the Chinese way and fended off their compliments.

After a while, my toes in the high-heeled shoes began to lose all sense of feeling. The glass globe lamps seemed to dim and brighten. Tian looked at me. "We need to leave," he said in Chinese. "You look tired." He turned to the other musicians. "We're going," he said. "I've got to get Min home in time to sleep. She is not—" he paused and struggled with his English "—she's not one of us crazy musician types."

"Don't leave so soon! Come and have a beer," said John.

Tian shook his head. "No, we should really be getting home."

We waited through a moment of silence. Then the redheaded woman said, "Come on, Tian. Don't be a *par*ty-pooper." Her green-shadowed eyes widened as she spoke.

John said, his voice still cheerful, "Liddy is right."

"No," Tian repeated. "Min is tired."

"I—okay," I said. It had begun to seem that we would lose face if we didn't go.

Tian turned to me. "I know you," he said, in Chinese. "You're tired."

"No secret codes allowed! What did you say to her, Tian?" Lydia demanded. Her face loomed close: the pale bright eyes, the freckles faintly glowing under a coat of powder, the slash of lipstick, orange in the light.

We all stood for a minute, and then I said, "It *is* okay." My voice cracked against the words. They fixed their eyes on me.

"Come on," said Tian. He took my arm and pulled me around the corner, to the coatrack.

"I'm not that tired; I could have gone out with them." I relaxed as I slipped into the familiar Mandarin language, thoughts forming easily again. "Why did you want to leave so much?"

Tian put his arm around me. "We don't need them," he said. "Aside from John, they're not my friends. I want to go home." I leaned into him. I could smell sweat, feel a deep heat rising from beneath his white shirt, and it was with some uneasiness that I realized he was happier than I had ever seen him.

That was when I blurted out, "Your playing scares me."

He laughed. "It's because of the way you are. It's why you're happy reading novels. You're only comfortable

with a piece of the world that you can hold in your hand."
I considered my hands, small and ordinary in black wool
gloves. Tian laid his cheek against my hair. "I don't mean
to hurt your feelings," he said. "Sometimes I'm afraid of
music, too. I think that's the reason I married you."

We found our coats and left the hall, walked into
the clear winter night, where the lights from the taller
buildings surrounded us like stars. Tian took my arm.
The pain in my feet vanished, and we walked toward the
subway stop.

"When I get promoted," Tian said, "we'll move to
Manhattan, and then I'll be able to spend more time at
home."

"Professor Sung."

"Professor Sung. Professors' wives don't take the
subway. You'll ride heated cabs everywhere."

"I'll get into a cab whenever I'm bored and want
something to do."

"And you'll never snap another bean," Tian added,
pointing at the Vermilion Palace, across the street. Its neon
sign glowed red.

"Did Spaeth say anything to you afterwards?" I asked.

"Oh, he got up and left right away. He always does that."

"He never goes out to have a drink with his students?"

"He is antisocial."

"So it is acceptable to be antisocial?"

"I never thought about it," he said. "I suppose so.
Why do you ask?"

We were at the top of the subway stairs. I reached
into my coat pocket for our tokens. My gloved fingers
touched an object there, something smooth and narrow
and heavy. I pulled it out and held it under the streetlight.
It was a tuning fork.

"What?" I stopped walking. "How did this get here?"

Tian took the fork; it glinted in his palm. "Who knows?" he said. "This is a nice one."

He struck the fork on his knee. "Hold still," he said, and he set the base knob on my forehead.

I stood still. I could feel it, like a current running all the way down my spine and between my legs, the powerful tiny thrumming of a perfect "A."

Tian put his gloved hands on both sides of my head, and kissed me where the tuning fork had been. I heard in his laugh a fierce recklessness. He dropped the fork into his pocket. "A gift from heaven," he said. I heard the powerful rush of the train, like a monster rumbling deep below. He grabbed my arm and we ran down the stairs.

I WAS quick-witted in those days, versatile and sly. If Tian ate a little less dinner one day, I would take care not to serve that dish again. He did not like our downstairs neighbor, Mrs. Lici, so I avoided her. One afternoon, we went for a walk in the park and I noticed him staring at a little boy. I threw a penny in the wishing-pond; I hoped our child would be a boy.

It mattered more to please him than to understand him. But as time went on, I wondered why he felt the way he did.

He had strong feelings about many little things. He insisted that we keep the chopsticks in a certain drawer. The forks and spoons went in another. And he had a special idea as to the rhythms of our days. Mornings must begin with a bowl of porridge, fermented tofu, and *youtiao*, a fried bread that I learned to pick up regularly in Chinatown. Over these dishes he would smile and joke. Evenings were another story. Often he would drift into a silent melancholy. He would sit in his small armchair, watching the patterns made from the setting sun through a wave in the window glass. This moody distance grew worse after his recital.

A few nights after the performance, he stopped by the restaurant to pick me up on his way home. When he had finished at school he often came by the restaurant and waited for me, helped us finish our work by snapping beans or peapods. As I worked the register, I watched him sitting with the men at the corner table around an enormous steel bowl of beans. Da Dao made a joke and Tian responded with a remark that made them all laugh. Seeing this I felt an odd sense of relief. For a moment I believed that he could be just like the others; he was one of the others.

"Your husband is a neat and hardworking man," said a waitress.

"*Nali,* that's in no way true," I said, to be polite. If only he could be so simple.

I wanted to tell her that I lived with a stranger. As we walked out of the Vermilion Palace, into the floating night city, I could not sense the shape and location of his soul. Only when he performed; only then had I truly seen my husband. What I saw had frightened me. But aside from that performance, I could not see any further.

I tucked my hand in his arm; we kept walking. He treated me kindly; he did not refuse to help at home. In fact, he was fussy about it. He wanted a role in things domestic, down to the placement of the furniture. He had a plan about where each piece would go. The bed must be pushed against the wall, so we would catch the light at a certain angle. We must enter and leave the bed from the left side. This interest in our house, although it should have comforted me, left me more confused. He was so exacting, but he did not explain why he wanted things the way he did. I wondered if it had to do with feng shui and the old superstitions; I considered the idea that he might believe in these things, despite his statement to the contrary.

Since the day of Tian's recital, I had been waiting to tell him he would become a father. I had dreamed of this, planned for this; he had not objected to those plans. Why was it then, I wondered, that I did not want to tell him? I had waited until after the recital, but afterwards I had still held back. Surely, I thought, there would be a time when I could share this news with a feeling of absolute certainty, security, and happiness. Would it not be tonight?

We boarded the subway train.

"How was your practice session?" I asked.

He shook his head. "Still unreal. Everything is unreal. I feel empty—the way I imagine a woman must feel after she has had a child."

I opened my mouth, and shut it. Finally I said, "Surely that must be a good feeling, then."

"I don't imagine so," he said. "All that waiting, hoping, building. There is bound to be an emptiness after such an experience."

He spoke casually, conversationally.

At home, undressing in front of our closet, I turned to him and told him, "I am pregnant."

He was unbuttoning his shirt. He looked up, stared at me, but my statement did not stop his clever fingers. Why were my own hands suddenly clumsy?

"Congratulations," he said.

"Are you happy?" I asked. I slid between the soft, cold sheets.

He got into bed and put his arm over my shoulders. "Yes."

This ended our discussion. The next day, he came

Hunger

home for dinner even more silent than usual. Had I put too much soy sauce in the chicken? Hopefully, I brought him a bottle of beer and watched him drink it down. But it made no difference. Finally, after dinner, I could not be silent. We sat side by side in our cloth-covered armchairs. I asked him, "Do you not want children? Is that the problem?"

"It makes you happy."

"And you?"

"I have always thought that I would someday have a child. But after this child is born, I think you should go to the doctor again. To ask for one of those things."

"What do you mean?"

Silence. When he spoke, he said very gently, "I think we should put off having a second child until we're sure we're ready."

"What is wrong?" I cried. "What's bothering you?"

He was sunk in contemplation of the wooden floor. "There is nothing bothering me."

"Please," I said. "You must tell me." I felt ashamed; it was like begging. I only wanted him to take me in his arms. But instead he drew back in his armchair, frowning to himself, as if he were making a deal with whatever powers that held him back.

"This is a story that I shouldn't tell, but I'll tell you, since it's important to you. I won't tell you much. Just enough so you can understand that it has nothing to do with you."

He stopped as if to rest. I did not like the words "It has nothing to do with you." I knew they were words I would remember.

"Everyone," he began again, "has things they want to do in their lives. But sometimes there is only one thing—one thing that a person *must do*. More than what he is told to do, more than what he is trained to do. Even more than what his family wants him to do. It is what he hungers for."

I sat frozen, listening to the distant patience in his voice.

"I was brought up to be a scientist. To stay in China and help my family. From the beginning, it was assumed that I would do this."

To stay in China, to help the country—these were the goals all good young men in those days had wanted. "I understand—"

"No," he said, and the vein in his jaw stood out. "You cannot understand."

There was a long silence after this.

Finally he said, "On the evening I left home, my father would only say one thing. 'You forget about us,' he said. 'If you truly want to leave us, to leave this home, to desert your country, then this family is no longer your family. I am no longer your father. You have no right ever to think of us.'"

The sun had slipped away; his face had disappeared in the dusk. "So I don't," he said. "That was the bargain. I left them, and I do not think of them any more. But I know that there is only one thing in life that I can permit myself to do. Anything else—frightens me. I am not allowed to have it."

For half an hour, we sat in the dark. "Now let us never talk about this," he said.

I had grown up on Taiwan with my mother and my father, until his death. We lived quietly, far away from the worst of the war and the turmoil of what happened after. I had been too young to remember much of anything. I had feared only the mail, the letters fragile and white, as thin as tissue. Their news was never hopeful, never good. Sometimes after we received mail, I would look behind the house and see my mother crying underneath the palm tree, holding a frail, white letter. When I asked her what had happened, she explained to me that her family, some living and some buried in the earth of China, was being destroyed—driven far and wide, or killed, our village taken over, the earth itself run over and destroyed. Her family blood flowed only through a few women now: through my mother and aunt, and me. And I had understood that there could be nothing as precious as children and the thread of family blood.

Tian did not discuss his childhood again. He never mentioned what had happened to his parents, how he had managed to flee the north and head to the coast, when he was just a teenager. I knew only what I could gather from his tastes: that his family had been educated, cultured, passionate. I assumed his parents had supported and indulged, up to a point, his love for music, but I also knew that this kind of family, this kind of faded scholars' class, had suffered when the Communists came to power. And I knew that the Communist government would not look favorably upon a family who had let a son run off to the West.

I began to see that all of Tian's specifications—the chopsticks, the breakfast food, the placement of lamps—were slips of willpower, signs of a forbidden loyalty to this other house that he had been barred forever from entering. Vigilantly, he fought against his memories of this house, but it could be called to mind by a simple trick of light, and it could not be forced away by sunshine or special food.

My mother would have said the dead were whispering in his ear, and although I did not believe in such things, I felt afraid. It seemed there were two Mins—an outer Min and an inner one. The outer Min looked plump with happy words and deeds; she had the round cheeks of a woman who would bear a child, a woman whose husband filled her with tender love. The inner Min starved; she woke in the middle of the night, then lay for hours wondering what was wrong. I wanted to call my mother, but decided against it on the excuse that it was too expensive. In reality, I did not want to admit to her that my marriage had come to this.

I fell asleep; my mother came to me in my dreams. I stood before her, small and sad, and she looked me over, as if counting my bones. She shook her head and beckoned me to sit with her and have a cup of tea.

"One wish," she said. "What would you see?"

I made my wish and looked down.

There it was, glimmering on the cup's round surface. I could see the simple courtyard house, similiar to many old Chinese dwellings. It had gray, slate tiles, wooden lattice windows lined with rice paper, and a small courtyard. Here was the spot where his parents liked to sit and watch the bees that lazed about his mother's apiary; here stood the table and bench where Tian had sat and learned his characters. I followed my vision through these rooms, absorbing every detail, every trick of light. I could feel a palpable sadness there, filtered through its walls.

I knew that I was seeing Tian's true home. Some part of him would always be there. I wanted to look into corners, underneath the furniture. I wanted to remember all the details of this vision, to create that house in this new world, but then I felt the vision fading, and the cup slipped from my hands.

My cry struck the walls and echoed back. Tian knelt over me, holding my face in his hands. "Min," he said. "Wake up. What is it?"

His voice sounded kind and tired, indifferent. I gasped, unable to hold it in, "You don't like it here! You'll go home. I know you will!"

We sat through a moment of silence. "No," he said. "I'll never go home." His arms loosened their hold on me.

I laid my ear against his chest and listened, knowing that my blurted words had cut him and could never be taken back. I kissed him and began to comfort him in the best way I knew how. We were silent and clumsy; our hands trembled. Tian's narrow kneecap nipped the inside of my thigh, and at this brief pain, I was filled with a sudden need to weep. I felt full to breaking, but I forced away my tears. I opened my eyes. A pale light lit the walls for a minute, a blink perhaps from the night's dark eye. I glimpsed Tian's face folded on itself, the vein that ran down his right jaw. I caught one glimpse before the pale light vanished and we were enveloped again in dark. I ran my hand over his throat. The feel of the vein—thick and smooth, like a scar—stayed in my fingers long afterward.

ON the morning of Anna's birth, Tian happened to be at school rehearsing for a chamber music concert. I took a taxi to the hospital and called him from the nurse's desk, but the baby came faster than his subway from Manhattan could. An easy birth, they said, and a healthy child, a healthy girl.

When I learned the baby was a girl I turned my head to the wall, feeling frightened and alone, as if even in this modern world the birth of a girl-child left me vulnerable, precarious. Tian said he didn't care about the baby's sex, as long as I had pulled through safe and sound. When the nurse left the room, he got into the hospital bed and held me, but despite this, despite the comfort of his words and hands, I could not shake my feeling.

We gave her the Chinese name of Anyu, Tranquil Jade, and the American name Anna. She grew intelligent and sturdy—a well-behaved first child. Perhaps the heavens took heed of my disappointment and produced a careful soul and body—sound and solid, taking no chances. She did everything exactly when the Chinese rhymes declared she would, flipping over at three months, crawling at eight, teething at nine with barely a murmur.

The Chinese also say that daughters take after their fathers, but whenever I looked at little Anyu I saw my own face. She had round bones, dusky skin, and brown eyes, as small and neat as almonds. Early on she began watching me and Tian and everything we did, as if she were trying to hold us in her gaze, to memorize us in case of future loss.

"Isn't she terribly serious for such a small child? Does she seem happy to you?" Tian asked one evening as we were sitting with the baby on the couch.

"Of course," I lied. "She laughs a lot when I take her to the playground. She loves to sit on the baby swings." But I wondered if Anna had dropped out from my shadow. Perhaps she could feel the fears I took such care to hide from Tian. She looked up whenever he stood to walk across the room, and when he left the room, she watched the door. When she learned to crawl, she started to follow him to the practice room, and I would find her sitting outside its closed door. I tried to reassure her, "Baba just needs to practice now. Baba will be back soon. Baba loves you." Sometimes my voice rang hollow, even to me.

Tian taught a music theory class that met at nine in the morning. In the first few months he slept in the back bedroom while I stayed with Anyu in our room, waking every few hours to feed her and silence her infrequent cries. I felt grateful when she learned to sleep through the night, so he could rejoin me in our bed.

As he had wanted, I had gone to be fitted for a diaphragm. I wondered if he had been ready for Anyu; I could not tell. He treated her fondly, but in a detached way, as if she really belonged to me. Perhaps he felt absorbed by work, where soon promotions would be announced. He spent so much of his time at school that I had to keep him up to date by phone.

"She said, 'Baba,'" I reported. "She asked for you."

"She knows who's boss."

"She stood up today," I told him a month later, when he called unexpectedly, during a rehearsal break.

"That's fine," he said. Then he added something I couldn't quite hear.

"What did you say?"

"I said I called to tell you I'm coming home early today."

"Don't you have another rehearsal?"

"Not tonight."

At five-thirty, I looked out the front window and saw him walking up the street as if pushing against a wind. Heavy shoes sounded on the stairs. I met him at the door.

"Well," he said, "I'm glad you're still here. I wanted to tell you my side of the story before you got wind of things." Then he laughed, as if he had just made a clever joke, but his face was gray, his forehead set in rigid lines.

"What do you mean?"

"I was 'passed over.'" Carefully, he sounded out the English words.

"What does that mean?" I asked as gently as I could.

"It means I didn't get the job."

"That's crazy," I said. "They must be crazy." I started to ask him exactly what they had said, but ate my words. I actually bit my tongue—I felt its muscle crunch between my teeth.

"They say they're aware of how much I'm contributing to the community and they hope that I don't go somewhere else just yet. They're offering me a few more years at this level. So I'll have another chance the next time a position comes up."

"That's good," I said.

"I'm old! I'm already older than most of them. I was already too old to start a career as a performer. If I can't make it now, when can I make it?"

"You're not old," I said. But I wondered. Although his hair remained thick and glossy, he wore an expression such as I had sometimes seen in men who had moved just barely past their prime: bewildered, as if they could not understand how the time had shifted under their feet.

Hours later, while we were getting ready for bed, he confessed to me that Lydia Borgmann and a male cellist had both been given jobs. And he told me the story that had been circulating in the department. This concerned the matter of Lydia's missing tuning fork.

Almost two years ago, at Tian's recital, a friend of Lydia's had returned the tuning fork she had borrowed for an orchestra rehearsal. Lydia was wearing a skirt with no pockets. She had run into the lobby and slipped the tuning fork into her coat before rejoining the audience. When she returned to the coatrack after leaving the reception, the tuning fork was missing. Then a few weeks later, during chamber orchestra practice, she had seen Tian produce that very fork from his violin case. It was a special German brand, which she doubted very much that he would have managed to buy himself, given the obvious condition of his finances.

"This is ridiculous," I said. "She obviously put her tuning fork into the wrong coat. She and I are about the same size, the coatrack was crowded, and we must both have been wearing black wool coats. How were we supposed to know that it was hers?"

"That must have been what happened," Tian said. But his voice was bewildered and vague. He sat on the bed, confused, slowly buttoning his faded flannel pajamas.

Hunger

"Did you tell them?"

"Well I—I couldn't think of what to say. I was so upset. And I had forgotten how you found that fork. To make things worse, Liddy never spoke to me about it when she saw it. That happened months ago. John found out eventually, and he told me."

I remembered the way Tian had refused to get a beer after his reception. What was it that had made me so uneasy? It was as if he were afraid to become a part of the music settlement. "Did you give it back?"

"Of course. She wasn't around, so I put it into her mailbox with a note. I was so upset. Maybe I should have waited and spoken to her. Maybe . . . " He had buttoned his pajamas wrong and had to start again.

"You need to go to school and act like nothing is wrong, tell them the story of my coat pocket as if it were a funny story."

"Maybe . . . "

I stared at his pale face, his fumbling fingers. "You're not guilty!" I cried. "Why do you look that way?"

"Maybe . . . "

I turned out the light, as if to shut off his thought, and got into bed. Surely the tuning fork was a small matter, but only in itself. It was their opinion of Tian that had been tarnished—or had he misunderstood the story? Certainly such a small thing would not cause enough suspicion against him to refuse a hire. More likely, I believed, it was only one matter in a series of small things—a culmination of drinks refused and other misunderstandings. I began to understand this, yet I also knew that I would not be able to explain this to him, to make him understand.

I remembered the night of Tian's brilliant recital—we had been so lighthearted, so happy, walking arm in arm through the sparkling street. We had inventoried our desires, caressing and counting them as if they were prayer beads. It must have been this admission of hope that had been our downfall. This great, forgetful happiness had led to what had happened. Why else would Tian have simply accepted the tuning fork as if it were a gift from heaven? I heard again Tian's reckless, almost angry laugh. He had wilfully forgotten that there was no such gift, that one should beware of any such gift. He had been greedy, careless. I thought of the tuning fork as it had lain in his palm, silver under the streetlight. I shivered.

"They're all so silly," I said to calm him, although my heart had pushed against my ribs. I put my hand on the back of his neck. "Let's forget about this," I said. "You're a harder worker and a more talented musician than any of them. It's only jealousy." I pulled him closer and ran my hand over his chest.

"Wait," he said.

"What is it?"

"You haven't put in your—"

I smiled in what I hoped was a distracting way. "I'm ready," I said, "for our son."

"No," he said. "No son."

There was a moment of silence. Suddenly I felt awkward, smiling at him like that. I lay back and drew the blanket over my breasts. "Why not?"

"We have Anyu. We don't need any more children."

I folded my arms underneath the blanket; I could feel the goosebumps there. I took a shallow breath. "No more?"

"Musicians can't afford children, you know," he said, and his voice held a light and bitter note that made me flatten into the bed. "Maybe you should have married a richer man."

That night I woke to the muffled strains of music. The

music drove me out of bed and into the foyer, where the air took on the smell of human sweat. I squinted through a crack near the hinge of the door to the practice room. In the silvery beams from the skylight I saw him playing, swaying desperately, enclosed in the little room. His shoulders and arms encircled the violin and bow as if he were about to crush them. His strong fingers hit the gleaming strings with audible force. His right arm drew powerful, seemingly interminable long notes, then convulsed as he struck deep chords near the frog. I feared he might snap something by pushing too deeply into the strings. I feared he would crush the wood in his hands.

Then his bow skittered off the strings. A single beam of light slipped down from the skylight, illuminating one wild eye. He knew I was there. He flung open the door. Did I seem as much of a stranger to my husband then as he did to me? I imagine how he must have seen me: a frightened woman, a stranger in cheap cotton pajamas with her hair smashed from sleep. "Go to sleep," he hissed. I hurried. I hurried back to our room and forced myself to drown in sleep before he returned.

The next morning Tian left early; he had a lesson to give at nine o'clock. I stood in the window and watched him leave, shoulders bent as if he were walking into wind.

I dressed Anna in her warmest clothes and took her for a walk. The carriage bumped on the broken pavement. Clouds hung low and hid the view; a sharp smell of snow filled the air. I had heard old women say that if a wife cannot bear a son, she will lose her husband. I did not believe in old women's sayings, but as I walked along and smelled the coming snow I began to understand them. They had been shared by generations of women who lay awake in anger and confusion, trying to understand how to make their husbands happy again.

"Mama," Anna was saying. "Mama, Mama." Guiltily, I stopped the carriage. Lately, she had begun to have specific fears; she saw menace in ordinary things: pigeons, headlights, faces in photographs. I knelt down and wiped a tear from her face.

"What is it?" I asked.

She examined my face with her small eyes and looked away.

I walked faster. I pushed the carriage to a little playground several blocks from home. Anna liked the bucket swing. I placed her in the swing and noted with relief the way her eyes began to shine, her plump legs to wave.

"Do you want more?" I kept asking. "More?"

I pushed her harder and higher. The quiet air filled with her shrieks of joy. I knew she would be tired and cross before her nap, but I did not stop. I pushed until I made myself dizzy, but I could not throw off the weight of fear.

She fell asleep on the way home. My arms were shaking as I lifted her from the carriage. I went to the closet and pulled out the cardboard box that I had not touched since Anna was born. My school papers, neatly filed away like fossil bones of my lost thoughts. I took out a folder and went through the papers, not stopping to read or try to remember. I was looking for a paper clip. When I found one I removed it quickly, tearing the page. I stuffed the folder back into the box and pushed the box back into the closet. Then I went into the bathroom and took out the round plastic case that held my diaphragm. I unbent the paper clip and made a tiny hole near the edge.

MY MOTHER DIED THAT YEAR. SHE WAS taken by a stroke that left her frozen for two days. On the third, she let out a wordless cry, sending her spirit from her mouth. Three thousand miles away, as I lay resting in Tian's easy chair, I jerked upright when the telephone rang. For a moment I thought I felt an echo of her voice.

I could not travel to Taiwan for the ceremony. The second child, the little fish in my belly, had grown too large for me to fly. My mother's sister buried her ashes. Afterwards, there came a flow of fragile white airmail letters. I remembered the way my mother had received such letters from China, years ago, how she had gone outside to read and weep under the great palm tree. Now the trail of white letters had finally come to me, and I wept also, understanding how alone she had been.

I had not seen my mother in many years, but I had written to her, and spoken to her by telephone when Anna was born. Now I had no one to tell things to anymore.

A few days later, Tian took Anna to the city for an evening concert. I left the apartment to buy some milk. It was growing dark when I returned. I walked up the stairs and past our second-floor neighbor Mrs. Lici, standing in her doorway, watching me from behind the security chain. She had been widowed several years before; her daughter came to visit every week and brought her gifts. She seldom used the stereo or the new color television. Instead, she chose to monitor the traffic near our brownstone, smoking, observing from her window.

I said hello to her and kept on up the stairs. But then she spoke, in a high, hoarse voice. I stopped and came back to the landing.

"I am sorry," I said. "What did you say?"

She looked me up and down.

"What's going on?" she rasped.

I tried to focus on her face, but I could not meet her insistent, pale eyes. "I'm sorry?"

"Who's the visitor?"

"No—no visitor."

"There was a woman," she said.

I shook my head.

She shrugged, and I walked past. As I continued up the stairs, I tried to forget about her question. Perhaps I had misunderstood her. But I knew what I had heard. For a moment I thought of thieves. I wondered if I should go back and knock on her door. But there would be no comfort from her.

The deadbolt had not been touched. Despite my relief at this, I felt a pressure on my throat. I left the door open and walked through each room, turning the lights on as I went.

My mother had often spoken of ghostly spirits who appeared after their physical forms had met the grave. Sometimes they were driven back to earth by a hunger for vengeance. But occasionally the ghost turned out to be a vast improvement over its mortal counterpart. She once told me a story she'd heard while making dumplings with her cousins, the story of a jealous wife, a hungry and uncertain woman, who clung to her husband with desperation. She was so possessive of this man that she peeled each piece of fruit for him, and when they went to visit friends and he joined a game of majiang she would stand behind him, keeping track of all his tiles, as if messages from another player, a woman, might be transmitted by this special means.

Then she died, giving birth to a stillborn child. To everyone's surprise, her husband fell into a bottomless sorrow. He had been a handsome and high-spirited man, and people had thought he might have been happy not to have her clutching him, but instead he grew gray and hollow-faced and spoke of her to anyone who would listen. He took to wandering through the park where she was buried. One morning he returned to work, cheerful, rested, and recovered. Eventually he chose another woman and they were married. When his friends asked what had brought him to recovery, he said, "She came to me, looking radiant and pale, and she said that I could do what I needed to do, that death had cured her of all but the most pure love for me, and what transpired on earth no longer mattered."

That night, after I made certain there were no visitors, I remembered my mother's story. A slow calm trickled through my bones. Perhaps my mother had not yet left; perhaps her spirit hovered somewhere about, waiting to say farewell to me. I decided I would wait for her. I sat for more than an hour in my easy chair next to Tian's empty one, my hands folded in my lap, staring at the shadowed room and waiting for her.

I had been an obedient child. I had wronged her only by growing into a woman and leaving her behind. Now she had left me, too, and perhaps this would equal things.

I could feel myself on sleep's delirious edge. My limbs jerked. Something pulled at me, pulled away from me. I thought I heard my mother's voice, calling, "Min!" And it seemed to me that I would only have to get on a plane and I would be able to see her again. I would rise, go into the bathroom, find the scissors I used for cutting Tian and Anna's hair. I would clip the curls of my permanent wave until my hair lay quiet, like a schoolgirl's. I would pack my green suitcase with the same things I had brought with me: a cotton sweater with embroidered marguerites, a patent-leather purse. Then I would climb into an enormous plane and rise into the sky. I could smell the wetness of the tropics. The warm, green scent soaked into my hair, my clothes, my skin.

For weeks afterward, I felt the tears come into my eyes, but I would not allow myself to cry unless Tian had left the house. I would get in the shower where even Anna could not hear me weep. In the closet, under my old books, I filled an envelope with cash. A dollar every week, even when we were at the bottom of the rice. After a year, I went to the bank and exchanged the pile for a fifty-dollar bill, but I never opened an account. I liked to have the money at hand. At night when I could not sleep, I would try to think of it, my secret. Sometimes I thought the money might be a way to escape. Sometimes it seemed like a way to keep us going. I added steadily to the pile and never touched it.

WHEN I went to give birth a second time, the doctor decided that he would have to cut me open to get the baby out. Something had made this second child turn sideways in my womb, as if it were undecided about entering the world.

The nurses reassured me the baby would suffer none of the trauma that usually took place in squeezing through the birth canal. Its features would be perfect, its skull round and smooth. And when I saw this child, it did seem clear to me that she had arrived quite differently from Anna—perhaps even from another mother. Her features looked so unlike mine. Her skin was white, her nose long, her mouth as red as a peony bud. She slept gravely, tiny nostrils moving with each breath. Even as an infant, she possessed an air of separateness. I watched her as she lay asleep and wondered what she concealed. I wondered, even then, if she had formed some judgment on me.

"Look at her," I said to Tian, when the nurse first put Ruth into his arms. "She doesn't resemble either of us. She doesn't look like my mother and father, either. Who is she?"

Tian did not answer. He stood there holding the baby, absorbed in each feature of her face. His lips parted in recognition and a kind of eagerness.

"What is it?"

"She resembles my family."

Afterwards it was as if he had never mentioned this. I would try to bring it up. "Look, she has such pale skin." Or, "Look at the shape of her hairline, a little peak like a point in a wave." But he never encouraged me.

He would sit and hold the baby for hours, his face dreamy and tender and innocent. I watched, and breathed more slowly. He did not want a son. He loved this child. I had not made a terrible mistake. In the following weeks, as I recovered from the surgery, Tian woke to go to Ruth each time she cried out in the night. And Ruth knew he would do this; from the very beginning she fussed and cried with the certainty of a daughter who knows she is essential to her father's happiness. I lay in the dark and told myself I was lucky things had turned out the way they did. And if I felt slighted by his attention, if I felt slighted by Tian, or jealous of my own child, I never admitted it, so great was my relief.

Anna said very little on the subject of her sister's birth, but one morning a few weeks after Ruth was born, she came up to me as I stood over the crib.

"Mama," she said. "Is the baby a dream?"

"No, she's not a dream."

"Sometimes I have dreams and when I wake up, they go away. I think Ruth might be one of them, Mama."

"I don't think so."

She said nothing, but for the rest of the morning, she followed me around the house, and she would not let go of my shirttail.

I hold this memory of Anna and Ruth as children. We had taken the train to Coney Island for a rare Sunday outing. We strolled on the boardwalk, hand in hand. Anna walked carefully, clinging to me, her eyes on her feet in order to avoid the cracks and keep her shoes unscuffed. But Ruth let go of her father and ran ahead, shouting at seagulls, leaping with the rhythm of the low waves rolling to the shore. Each step light, poised and sure, as if she had been born with a special awareness of the balance between gravity and flight. I had tied pink ribbons on the ends of their braids—Anna's bows quivered stiffly in the wind, while Ruth's flew bedraggled behind her. Tian stayed behind with me and Anna, but now and then his hand jerked slightly in mine, as if he were about to follow Ruth and only his sense of duty kept him on the ground with us.

TIAN did not allow Anna to pick up a violin until her fifth birthday. By that time, she had been watching him since infancy; she was as eager as he was. Even before the violin, when she had only been permitted to hold a toy he had constructed with a ruler and a margarine box, she had practiced when Tian was away from home, climbing on a chair in the bathroom so she could watch her left wrist in the mirror. He had told her to be careful that it did not collapse inward. The most basic human reaction, he said, would be to clutch the violin's neck. At meals, she spent more hours pressing her fingertips into the tablecloth, an exercise that Tian had promised would strengthen the muscles around her double joints. She had long, narrow-tipped fingers, just like his, and he taught her to train them the way an athlete trains her body—gradually, continually, taking note of its flaws and strengths in learning.

Watching her, I saw she found a pleasure in this relentlessness. Even more, it was a way of getting Tian's attention. His tired mouth grew firm again whenever he saw her testing her fingers on the dinner table. Manners came second. Everything came second. Anna understood this naturally, unlike Ruth, who greedily drank her sweet porridge to the bottom of the bowl, who watched cartoons after school instead of listening to concerti. Ruth would curl into the faded couch, her shining eyes fixed on the television in absorption and belief.

One morning Tian and Anna emerged from the practice room after a triumphant lesson. She stood proudly in the kitchen and performed a new piece, the clear, plaintive notes from her small violin ringing through the quiet kitchen. She smiled shyly when I applauded from behind the ironing board. Afterwards Tian put on his coat, picked up his own violin, and headed for the door. From my place in the kitchen I watched him pause in the foyer and look into the living room where Ruth sat watching cartoons on television. Ruth sensed him standing there and flicked her gaze away from the screen. She scooted down into the sagging couch, pulling up her t-shirt to expose her belly button, daring him to tickle her. He set down his instrument. Solemnly, slowly, he came forward. She allowed him to tickle her, squirmed and giggled until Tian's mouth twitched.

"Mushroom head," he said finally. "Rice bucket." She flipped in his arms like a fish so that her legs kicked over the back of the couch and her head hung over the seat. She gazed at him upside-down. Her mouth hung open in delight, her eyes gleaming, filled with greed and with his love.

Anna worked at the violin to earn this love that came so naturally to her sister. But I knew about other reasons that she found such comfort in music. She had trouble in school. Her intelligence had proven itself through her quick progress in games and math, but she possessed no background in English. The teacher explained to Tian that she seemed afraid of the other children, stood apart and watched their gestures and expressions as if she could not hear.

The failure was all mine. I buried myself in Chinese

novels and read the Chinese newspaper; my Chinese had formed a brick wall in my mind and only short sentences and stray phrases of English could slip through the cracks. I vowed to study my old books. I would sit for hours staring at the simple sentences on the page. *The butter is on the table. The cat is under the bed.* But none of the new words I learned seemed able to express my thoughts—I felt as if, in order to speak English, I would have to change the climate of my soul, the flavor of my tongue. I told Tian to speak to the girls in English, which he did when he had the time, but often, when he returned from a difficult day at work, we would lapse into Chinese at the dinner table, exhausted and relieved, as if we were falling into each others' arms.

Eventually the problem solved itself. One afternoon, Anna came home from school and I greeted her at the door as usual, asked her about her day. But her eyes darted past me to focus on her sister. Ruth stood behind me on her sturdy child's legs, a necklace of purple plastic beads dangling from her fist. They were Anna's beads. We had bought one necklace for each, pink for Ruth and purple for Anna, but Ruth had misplaced hers almost immediately.

Anna had walked out the door that morning with her "school face" on—nervous and withdrawn, a mute child. But now she stood rigid, transformed by rage.

"That's mine!" she cried. I stopped in the middle of locking the door; the English words sounded so fierce and strange as she claimed them.

"No!" Ruth cried right back at her in English. "Mine!"

"Give it to me!"

Anna seized the necklace; Ruth pulled, and the string of beads exploded, hailing on the kitchen floor. Anna howled—a sheer animal cry of no language—a howl so filled with pain and rage that Ruth scurried from the room. I put dinner aside and spent half an hour crouching on the floor with Anna, looking behind chairs and tables and in corners, coaxing the tiny balls from behind the furniture.

From that day on, my daughters spoke to each other in English only. Ruth had picked up a large vocabulary from watching so much television. By the time she left home for kindergarten, she was virtually fluent.

It was sometime shortly after Ruth started school, during both girls' winter vacation, when Tian arrived home early again. This time I was sitting with both girls in front of the television. I heard his key turn in the lock and jumped up to go to the door. Tian's face was pale, and he smelled of the cold and melting snow.

"I have to talk to you," he said.

"What is it?"

"Not in here." He motioned to Anna, who stood big-eyed, listening, in the doorway. Her wide eyes were riveted in terror on the tired man, her father.

"Mama and Baba are going for a walk," I said. I hurried to the closet for my winter coat. "We're only walking around the block. Will you make sure Ruth stays here with you until we get back?"

Anna nodded, her face fixed with a desperate obedience. I pulled Tian out of the door. We went down the two flights of stairs, past Mrs. Lici's scowling face behind the chained door, then out of the building. I took deep breaths of the cold air.

"Tell," I said.

"Dean Spaeth came into my office."

The dean had finally told Tian that he had outlived his usefulness in his current position. The department had an obligation to let younger graduates teach at this level. After spring semester he would no longer have a place.

"They said I can't teach theory. They said the students have trouble with my English. They said my English has not improved and they don't think they will be able to wait for it."

"Your English is fine," I said. "And who needs English to teach music? They're just making some excuse." But I remembered the way he stumbled over his sentences when speaking to strangers. I knew that if they had really wanted to hire him, they would have mentioned his English earlier. They would have made suggestions. We would have been able to prepare.

At some point in his time at the music school, someone had decided he would not be hired for a permanent job. But they had failed to tell him this. They had held onto him while knowing they had no place for him. And now where would he go? Without the school, we had no money and no green card.

We walked in silence, breathing white steam in the chilly air. I thrust my hands deep in my jacket pockets and curled them into fists, fighting an unaccountable anger at my husband. He had been unable, or unwilling, to assess the truth about his standing at the school. How could he have kept on, dogged, never changing his approach, never willing to fit in, without knowing that he would not be chosen? Or had he, somehow, understood all of this? Expected it? Wanted it? The resignation in his shoulders made me wonder if all along he had been hoping to fail.

Tian spoke, as if guessing my thoughts. "A punishment," he said. He paused and grasped my arm. "A punishment, not for this, but because I asked for more than I was meant to have, because of years ago—"

"Stop it!" I said, much too loudly and too angrily. His hand dropped to his side.

We approached our brownstone. I looked up at our apartment and saw Ruth's face in the window. For some reason I felt surprised by the sight of her behind the glass, like a doll in the window of a grimy dollhouse. She had a doll's expression: porcelain, lovely, inhuman. She did not seem to see Tian or me, but instead looked past us, down the street. I turned to Tian. He stood on the uneven sidewalk, his brown, lined face tilted toward the window, looking up at her as if he had just awakened from sleep and was remembering, for a moment, his interrupted dream.

COMING over from Taiwan, Tian had listed his occupation as "student." He had brought a letter of introduction from a man named Ma, an internationally renowned violinist. He had earned a visa sponsorship after auditioning at the music school. Now we had lost our official sponsor.

We had entertained some hope that he might find a job at a junior college. But along with everyone's, our luck had run dry. After years when almost any holder of a master's degree could find work at a university, there had come a glut of graduate students. All over the country, Ph.D.'s were being turned away from teaching jobs and being forced to look for other work.

Tian's friend John heard of a job in Minnesota, a job directing the orchestra at a private high school run by a friend. But when Tian mentioned this job to me, I could only think of my flight from San Francisco to New York, which I had boarded upon arrival from Taipei in early April. We had stopped in Chicago to refuel and pick up passengers. As we had circled, ready to land, I had seen miles upon miles of fields filled with snow, broken only by fences and occasional rows of dead cornstalks. When the new passengers stepped onto the plane, enormous, with their giant hands, talking loudly and exclusively in English, I had shivered into my seat and wondered what New York City would be like. Now I thought about living in a place near Illinois. I shivered again, but I knew that I would do it, if it meant putting our family into secure hands.

"It is a job," I said.

Tian frowned. "I don't want to teach high school students," he said. "I would rather not work in music at all."

I remembered my mother's warning that I should keep attending English classes.

In the end, we turned to the only people we knew who had the means and willingness to help us. The summer after Tian finished his job, years after I had left the place, we took the subway to upper Broadway and walked to the Vermilion Palace.

The restaurant had grown older. The globe-shaped lights had darkened to a dim yellow. The dragons on the wall had been disfigured by a water stain. We went to the office in the back, through the orderly but aging kitchen. My old manager, Da Dao, had bought the place. He had withered, it seemed to me; his neck had shrunk, his hands were thin, but his generous nose was still red, I noticed. So he was still inclined to take a drink when the days grew long. He remembered me. He clapped my arm in a gesture that echoed some old complicity we had shared.

I told him Tian needed a job.

For a moment, Da Dao stood with his arms at his side. His eyes wandered over the kitchen floor as if he were looking for the right thing to say, and when he found it, his relief lifted his pale eyebrows.

"Well, it depends on what kind of work he needs," he said. "We're soon to be overstaffed with chefs. My wife's brother is arriving from Taiwan."

He paused. I realized that Tian was not going to reply.

"He doesn't cook," I said.

Da Dao's phantom eyebrows lifted higher. "Well, if

that's the case, we're all in luck. One of the busboys just left to go to college." He said it didn't matter that Tian could not cook. He could help by bussing dishes until he learned to chop up meat and vegetables. He would work from eleven until ten, six days a week. The restaurant was closed on Mondays.

"A dollar an hour, plus a share of tips," he offered. "That's twenty-five cents more than the restaurants downtown."

Through all of this, Tian stood quite still. He had never paid much attention to food. He didn't know the names of vegetables; pork or chicken tasted the same to him. He sometimes had to be reminded to eat more than a single bowl of rice; he had a habit of simply sitting at the table, not even thirsty, with the light carving shadows into his face.

I thanked Da Dao. As we walked out, I caught the eye of a woman I had once been friendly with, a waitress. I smiled, and she nodded back with some confusion, trying to remember if she had seen me, or someone like me, in the past.

We retraced the familiar route back to the subway.

"Well, that will do—just for now," I said.

Tian did not meet my gaze. He had earned three dollars per lesson at the music school.

"When Ruth gets old enough for school, I can work part-time and you will have more time to practice." I waited a minute. "Tian?"

"I'm sorry. What did you say?"

I had planned to say to him, "I'm sure you'll find a job in music." But I could not say it. I did not know if I would believe myself. He walked beside me, his eyes fixed on the busy street. I remembered the first time I had seen him in the restaurant. He had looked at me and made me warm. Why could I not do the same for him? Now, as we approached the corner of 96th Street, I saw his eyes flick sideways. I wondered if he was searching for relief in the form of a Checker cab, if he wanted to speed downtown to a bridge and leave me, and our daughters, standing at the subway station. We reached the intersection. I put out my hand to stop him. We stood together, waiting for the light to change.

"I'm sorry," Tian repeated. "What did you just say?"

"I was going to say—" I thought quickly "—that with this job you can still practice with Anna in the morning, before she leaves for school at nine."

For a while he considered this. He looked at me and nodded. "That is true."

Tian stayed at the Vermilion Palace. He did not advance to the wok, and he did not seem to care. When he came home at night, his hands and arms ached, and he could not practice. But still, things had not reached their worst. I made plans to run the household while working part-time in my old job. We managed to cover our expenses. Anna had found a way to flower beneath her father's eye. It seemed to me we went through a quiet year. Then there came a day I do not like to remember.

At a certain stage, a violin student must free her left hand from its fixed "first position" at the bottom of the fingerboard and slide the left hand up the neck, shortening the strings and forming higher and higher notes. This movement into "higher positions" enables the violinist to achieve a remarkably wide range of tones, higher than most instruments, by stretching her hand almost to the top of the fingerboard. Anna began to learn the higher positions shortly before her seventh birthday.

It was a Monday evening, and Anna and Tian were practicing in the kitchen as I watched them, ironing. They went through a few warm-up exercises and then it was time.

Hunger

Tian sat on a kitchen chair. Anna stood with her violin scroll thrust directly under his eyes. Then she slowly released her hold at the bottom of the fingerboard and began to move her hand.

"Right," Tian said. "Just slide your hand. Try third position." Third position, I knew, meant that she would move her first finger, or index finger, up the fingerboard to the place where the third had been. This, he told her, was the note "A." She drew her bow and I listened to the changing tones of her finger sliding higher up on the narrow E string.

"When do I stop?"

"Try to listen for the note."

She paused. "What do you mean?"

"Listen for the A." The three of us all listened to the sliding sound. I heard what sounded like the right note. But Anna did not stop. "Stop now," Tian said. "Do you hear it? Do you feel it?" He hummed an A. His singing voice had always surprised me with its delicate rich tenor.

Anna slid past the note; I could hear it myself. Her finger stopped sliding. "Yes," she said firmly, screwing up her face and closing her eyes. "I think I hear it." But as I watched her face, I felt the terrible sensation written there, the sensation of bumping up against a wall in the dark. She did not understand his question. What was she supposed to hear?

"Try again."

Anna brought her hand down to first position and slowly slid it up again. Her eyes were fixed on his face, searching, watching his expression for the right note. There it was: a flicker of recognition in his eyes. But she stopped moving her hand an instant too late.

"Too high," Tian said. "Too high. Try again."

"Can I stop?" she asked. "My arm is tired."

He looked up at her. How I knew by then the discomfort of being fixed with those dark, unblinking eyes. He had a way of looking at people as if he were envisioning them at another moment in time, the future, but there were also moments when he stared blankly, as if reeling from the truth. Now his eyes had no expression at all. Anna had never asked to stop practicing before. "Of course," he said. She turned, her shoulders dragging, and put her violin back into its case. Her "Beethoven" t-shirt looked dark with sweat. She walked away with her hands thrust deep into her pockets.

That was the first day. Over the next few weeks, as I listened to Anna practice by herself after school and in a few brief sessions with her father, I began to understand the nature of her limitation. She had a mediocre sense of pitch. She had trained herself to hear up to a certain point, but she could not sense the spot where the desired note sang out clearly, sweetly, without dissonance. As she slowly learned this fact about herself, she no longer looked at her fingers or pressed them on the table at meals. The ritual of practicing lasted longer. She said she wanted to surprise him. But her fingers had lost their magic, had grown cool and limp with fear, and this coolness spread into everything she touched. I could see it in Tian's glance. It seemed sometimes that he would barely look at her.

Some nights I vowed to speak to him. I rubbed my skin with lotion and changed into my best pajamas, determined to say or do something, anything, to stop that wave of disapproval. But Tian would emerge from the bathroom, weary, damp from his attempts to wash the smell of restaurant oil out of his skin, and I would find myself unable to speak. We would turn out the light and climb into our separate sides of the bed. I remember that as a time of mourning for all the things that we had lost: our expectations; Tian's job; my body, which I had noticed changing in the mirror, which had begun to lose its agile, thoughtless grace. Some days, I felt as if I were struggling through water. My arms and legs grew so heavy I could not move, and I had to concentrate on every breath.

I felt afraid of further testing Tian. It seemed to me that when he looked at Anna he saw nothing but his own struggle; he hated her difficulties, but he especially hated his own. He seldom practiced, in those days, and when he did his fingers seemed slower, his music thinner. No, I could not talk to Tian.

Around that time, Anna began to learn the second violin part of a double concerto by Bach. It had been Tian's hope that Ruth and Anna would someday be able to play this together. She took it on, I think, as a final hope, and when she announced her plan to me I nodded and smiled, as if I fully believed that she could do anything to please him. As if he were still capable of being pleased. She applied her precise memory to the intricacies of Bach. There were several weeks of hope and high expectations. But as I listened, I could tell that the more she learned, the less the notes seemed to make sense to her. Their patterns were intricate, evasive, hard to hold in the mind. Each new section of the piece seemed to layer difficulty on the last, bringing out new weaknesses in her, relentless, stubborn weaknesses that were revealed day by day. The first movement alone contained a number of "shifts" to second and third position. She found third position difficult, but second even more so.

One Saturday evening, I happened to walk by the practice room to put away some freshly ironed laundry. Tian sat at the piano, trying to help her sound out a jungle of minor arpeggios. Something in his attitude made me pause there in the foyer. He lifted his hands from the keys and said in a barely audible voice, as if speaking to himself, "Go away."

Anna stopped in the middle of a bowstroke. "What?"

"Go away," he said. He closed the piano and folded his arms on top of the lid. Then he put his face into his arms.

I watched as Anna went to her violin case and wiped her instrument down. After she closed the case she paused, afraid to talk to him, waiting for him to speak. He refused to look up. His spine seemed tense and rigid, coiled there, defiant. I had seen him that way a week ago, closing the checkbook after paying the bills.

Anna walked into the kitchen, her expression numb. I went back to my ironing. I usually worked there during their practice sessions, pulling the laundry line in from the fire escape, collecting the rows of plaid and chambray shirts, and pressing them carefully, although by the time Tian came back from the restaurant each night his shirts were stiff with sweat and oil and food stains. Anna watched my hands—fingernails trimmed short, pink-edged from the heat of the iron. Small and sturdy hands, completely unremarkable.

Anna's little face was absolutely stoic. For a moment I felt the way I did on winter mornings, watching Tian leave for work. I would see him close the door, three stories below, and walk down the glowing, snowy street into the long gray day, wearing his freshly-ironed shirt and old winter coat, heading for the subway station. As I looked at my daughter's face, I began to understand that to love another was to be a custodian of that person's decline—to know this fate, hold onto it, and live.

"Do you want a snack?" I asked.

"No."

I finished a shirt and tried again. "Would you like to help me fold?"

There were three baskets of whites behind the iron-ing board. After she had finished one of them, we heard Tian's footsteps in the foyer.

"Ruth!"

There was no answer. He called again. We heard the television shut off and Ruth dragging her sneakers into the foyer, then up onto the slightly elevated, sound-proofed floor of the little room.

They left the door open. I listened as Ruth tuned her strings. She had already grown as tall as Anna, and her reach was slightly longer, so at that time they shared a violin. The violin, a half-size, had been outfitted with little steel fine-tuners, like all childrens' instruments, but Ruth had learned to affect the manner of profession-al violinists, deep-tuning from the wooden pegs at the scroll. She must have picked it up from Tian and from being forced to watch the Boston Pops. This pretension was one of the things about Ruth that made Tian smile and roll his eyes. As she listened to her sister's tuning, Anna's small brown nose wrinkled over her laundry. I had always ignored it, but today I listened as Ruth drew long bowstrokes through the sweet slant and curl of sliding pitch.

"Enough," Tian said.

She had been playing now for six or seven months. She had raced through the early pieces with little enthusi-asm and horrendous posture, her left hand welded into a vise-grip, clutching the neck when it was supposed to hang free and away, her instrument jammed under her chin at an unnatural angle. She had a tendency to grow tired during practice and to rest her left arm against her side, the violin drooping. She played carelessly, with a tendency toward sloppy fingering, and sometimes when she was frustrated and Tian asked her to repeat something she would stick out her bottom lip, push her bow down on the little violin, and play the section he wanted in horrible, rough squeaky tones. Sometimes this irritated him, but usually he just laughed and shook his head. I imagined her now in the practice room, frustrated and bored, standing in front of Tian, a picture of childish disobedience and frustration.

I began on another of Tian's shirts. My head felt light, my hands slow.

Anna said, "Why does Baba let her learn new pieces? She has horrible tone." Anna had been pointed out to her sister as a model in these things. She had often been praised for her focus and industry, but still Ruth had been allowed to move on.

Today she was learning a simple Brahms waltz. She was having problems with the waltz rhythm and with the two-note slur, which required her to hold out a long note, conserving bow space.

"Try again," Tian said. "One, two, and-three-and—"

She stopped playing. "I don't get it, Baba," she said, her voice childishly sweet. "Can we do something else?"

"No," he said. Usually he humored her, but on this night I could hear a tremble in his voice, as if his breath were thin and stretched around a great bubble of emotion. The clapping and counting began again. I listened to the tune strain and wobble as she struggled to hold out the note.

"Again."

"One, two, and-three-and—" Again her notes wobbled as she ran out of bow.

"Fourth finger, fourth finger," he muttered. She had a habit of substituting her third finger for her weaker pinkie.

Ruth said, so quietly I could barely hear her, "Baba, I want to stop now." He kept clapping, ignoring her. "Please can we stop now?"

"No." Even when she was an infant, he had not refused her anything. Once he had walked across the Brooklyn Bridge with her on his shoulders so she could look over the rail at the water.

"Baba!"

Silence. The iron slipped in my wet hands. I could feel the air change, suddenly, like an intimation of foul weather, and then there came a sharp and monstrous *bang*.

He had struck the top of the piano. The strings inside its soundbox sang. "*You cry!*" he screamed. "*You cry!*"

"Baba, let me stop!"

"You go ahead and cry!" His voice broke and climbed upwards. "You cry all you want!" Again, the bang of his hand hitting the piano, in rhythm this time. "You cry! But—*play!* One, two, and-three-and one, two, and-three-and—Save your bow! Save your bow!"

As I ironed I watched Anna fiddle with the frayed towels that had once been pink but were now faded to a creamy white. Tian's threadbare pajamas. My own underwear, which I had scrubbed and washed until it was unraveling. Ruth's white cotton panties, identical to Anna's—Ruth would grow taller than her older sister, I realized at that moment. Anna folded steadily, not looking up at me. I opened my mouth but my throat was dry.

Once, much later, Anna asked me why I didn't inter-fere that night. This question came after she had taken two years of intensive Chinese, when she felt safe enough to look back at it all from the dry, protected shores of college psychology. Was I afraid of him, she wanted to know. Was I afraid he might abuse me with this sudden, vicious anger? Or perhaps Ruth was so spoiled that I felt this taking-down might be good for her? She *had* been terribly spoiled, Anna added, with some bitterness in her voice. What had I been thinking? I told Anna, Let's not talk about it now.

But I can still remember myself, a young and desperately hopeful woman, ironing a faded blouse and trying not to listen.

"I want to stop! Let me stop!"

"You cry! You cry!"

The ironing board creaked under the blunt iron.

"Baba! Baba!" Weeping.

"Do you understand? From now on, you work. You practice every day. Do you understand."

"*No no no no—*" Her voice rose to a shriek. There was a slam as he closed the door, and they were trapped inside the room together.

I could still hear muffled sounds. He clapped and counted. She played and cried. The night breeze flowed in from the window, pouring through me. I stood and tried to let my mind follow this escaping breeze, to enter the world beyond our house, and then despite my efforts I began to hear. I heard, above his banging and her wailing, the fragile, turning rhythm of a waltz. Their waltz was a thin tune from a small violin, sweet and wobbling, intricate in its pauses and plunges forward. But it was music. Somewhere through all this mad coercion ran a thread of beauty. I looked at Anna. She had heard it too. She sat with tears running down her face, clutching a pair of underpants, tearing it in her hands.

THERE was a hole in our house, like a great mouth, filled with love words and lost objects. How else could it have been explained? A stolen hat, a misplaced tuning fork. One child's joy and another's pleas for love. The hat, the happiness, the child's cries all vanished as if they had never been.

Tian had always been a private man. In our closest moments, he had always held something in reserve. The hope, the striving and occasional joy, had surfaced in his musical flight. It was not until he lost his job that I learned what was left over. It was as if the tender parts of him had burned away, coming down to earth, leaving a battered shell.

Several years passed. Five days a week, Tian went to work. He would shut the door so quietly that despite my vigilance I would sometimes fail to hear him. I would suddenly sense his absence, run to the window, shout goodbye. But my words disappeared behind him. All my hoping, the plans I creased into his crisp soap-scented shirts and trousers—all those wishes whirled away.

After Ruth entered school, I took a part-time lunch shift, in my old job as hostess. It seemed to me that the customers did not notice me, I paid so little attention to my surroundings. I came home in time to make the rice for dinner.

On Sunday and Monday after dinner, during the evening practice sessions, Anna would sit in the kitchen with me. Tian had made a rule of no more television; Ruth must not be tempted. Anna would study and I would work, trying not to listen to the sounds from the foyer, the scolding and the tears. We heard the struggle of commands and sobs, and increasingly over the years, the pure melody of the violin rising over all of it like a great rope of silk, smooth and shimmering, shot through with glints and shades of beautiful light. Often we sat all evening without speaking. Anna would not answer me when I spoke to her. We both knew she was my child now, my charge. We knew she did not want me.

Ruth grew tall and almost painfully slender; in the sixth grade, she began to practice on Tian's full-sized violin. At fourteen, she won a city-wide competition for young musicians. As the winner, she would perform a concerto, accompanied by the orchestra that had sponsored the competition. Tian had chosen the Sibelius concerto, and for many, many months he and Ruth practiced those wondrous loops of sound, the joyous slithering movements of Sibelius.

He treated her as cruelly as he did himself—with complete disregard for her age and temperament. But she did not complain to me or Anna. She would play and sob for hours, but emerge from the room without a word. She believed, she had known from infancy, that she held him in her hands. Now he had replaced his tenderness with this stern passion and she followed him there, believing the source of his sternness lay in love. In this blindness, I began to see, she and her father were alike.

All morning during summer vacations, plus two evenings a week, he sat in the tiny room for hours and helped her practice. I remember the way he looked at her when things went well: intense, prideful, the dispassionate yet hungry stare that I learned to recognize on television in coaches or trainers as they watch the taut bodies of their favorites. They exchanged few words; just an occasional "no," or "again," or "tone." "Bad fingering." "Again. Again." Ruth did not grimace or stop to complain. To this day I hold an image of them practicing under the skylight: Tian in the corner with his impenetrable and hungry gaze, and Ruth, stark-faced, her clear features lit gold or gray from above, lips pale and nostrils flared; her half-closed eyes, shadowed beneath. Her long-sleeved t-shirt flapped as she moved her arms.

Afterwards, she ignored me as she swept around the house, her full lips closed in a faint sneer, with an expression of great privacy. She had the ability to become impenetrable through sheer volition. She might sit in her room reading, or stare at the television for several hours before she would finally speak to me or Anna; when she came back to us, she would be tired and confused, like a sleepwalker who had walked into a wall and awakened with bruised eyes. She did, in fact, sleep badly—she had a tendency to lie awake or get out of bed and walk around the house.

One night she stumbled in the kitchen and we all woke to a howl and crash. The next morning, Tian questioned her sternly. "What were you doing?"

She looked confused. "I don't know."

"Were you walking in your sleep?"

"No."

"Well, next time, stay in bed!"

For a few weeks we listened carefully at night, but the problem had passed. I decided Ruth simply needed some time to be alone, to think. I thought that she must feel in need of an occasional peaceful moment, a moment in which she might be able to grow accustomed to the progress she made each day, the flight of her abilities so far above the level a fourteen-year-old's should be, the fact of her extraordinary talent. Her days were filled with school and practicing, carrying some enormous weight. It must be difficult to find some time to think, living as she was under the spotlight of her father's fierce attention.

One night, as Tian and Ruth practiced, as Anna read and I prepared the next day's vegetables, the clock seemed to tick more loudly than usual, and I looked up. Anna's small, dark eyes were fixed on me.

She had not grown more adventurous in adolescence—only sullen and withdrawn. Her features lacked the self-acceptance that might one day give her beauty or serenity. Now she frowned. She spoke in simple Chinese words, dull and halting. "You and Baba never talk about yourselves."

Her choice of language was a sign: she wanted to hear the truth about us. For some reason, this desire of hers left me uneasy. It is true that many Chinese people don't like to ask each other direct questions, but my uneasiness did not spring from the question only. Her interest also frightened me, reminded me that children form their own opinions.

"I didn't think you wanted to know," I said. I began to strip the tough outer fibers off a stick of celery, and I kept my eyes on the paring knife.

"I do want to know."

"What do you want to know about?"

She asked carefully, "You and Baba—why are you together?"

"What do you mean?"

"You and Baba—why did you marry?"

"It was *yuanfen*," I told her.

"What is that?"

I did not know how agitated I was until I felt the paring knife go too far and press lightly, in warning, against my thumb. I set down the knife. "*Yuanfen* is your fate."

I thought of my mother's words. "That apportionment of love which is destined for you in this world." But I could not explain this to Anna. She would not have understood the Chinese words. She was too proud to ask me to repeat myself. I did not know enough English to tell her what I wanted to say. I knew simple phrases. I knew how to say, "Put the rice on the table," or "Are you cold? Do you want more to eat?" But I had no words to say what lay in my heart.

Now a furrow darkened between Anna's heavy brows as she struggled to find words for the real questions, questions that would unleash some crucial secret she believed I understood. I held my breath.

"Why did you and Baba leave China?"

"Your father and I came over separately," I said. "We met each other and married here."

There was a pause while she comprehended this. "But *why* did you leave? And Baba?"

"I left because of the war. My parents decided to move. Taiwan was safer."

"But Baba?"

I thought about what to tell her. "Your father came over alone."

"Why?"

"He wanted to be a violinist."

From the practice room, we could hear a fairly smooth rendition of the concerto's third movement. Ruth learned notes and fingerings very quickly when she set her mind to it. I concentrated on this music, the quick, bright notes that fell and cascaded like water droplets.

"But why?" Anna cried. I looked up. She scowled; her eyes were full of tears. "Why is music so important?"

How many times had I asked myself this question? "I don't know," I said. "It's his desire. It's—it's part of his bargain with himself."

Anna stared at her hands.

I had seen a television show where the mother called her grown daughter "Honey" and comforted her in her arms. I stood up and walked around the table to where Anna sat. I put my arm around her rigid shoulders.

I asked her, "Are you cold? Do you want anything to eat?"

"Leave me alone!"

I sat back down. I looked at her bent head, her neat, black cap of hair, and remembered how I had turned my face to the wall when she was born.

TWO Saturdays before Ruth's performance, I took both girls to a rarely visited Manhattan department store. We rode the escalator to the hushed third floor, the women's floor, where the stifling air held the scent of brand-new merchandise mingled with heavy perfumes. Ruth took one happy glance around the place and disappeared into the racks of clothes. Anna stayed with me. She sat in the chair by the changing rooms, refusing to browse, although she, too, needed something to wear to the concert. I left her sitting there and went to search myself. I found what I thought was a suitable dress and brought it over.

"Try this."

"Do I have to?"

I gestured at the dress. I shook the hanger.

"What are *you* going to wear?"

I reverted to Chinese. "I'm not growing, like you. I don't need anything new."

Finally I persuaded her to try on a blue dress. She stood in the little room, self-conscious, unable to look in the full-length mirror.

"That is nice," I said. I pulled at her collar; she had made no effort to adjust the line or fall of the dress. She would not look at herself reflected next to me, would not meet my eyes because she knew how she resembled me. I was not ugly; I was not bad, but I was not what she would have liked to be.

I studied our reflections. No one seeing the two of us would fail to recognize that we belonged together. And why was that? I wondered—was it only our round faces, our dusky skin? Or was it written, indelibly, in our faces and our bodies, that we were not and would never be women who expected or felt that they deserved to be loved the most? And had I always been this way? I gazed at the mirror for a few more seconds before Anna scowled and turned away.

Finally she agreed to a dark-green jumper and a flowered blouse. As she changed back into her jeans, I heard Ruth's high voice calling from a dressing stall.

"Ma?"

"Where are you?" I asked.

"Just wait a minute. I'll come out."

She emerged a few minutes later, wearing a sleeveless, scarlet A-line gown.

"Where did you find that dress?"

"Not yet—I'm not ready. You have to zip me up."

She turned around and lifted her heavy hair, exposed the white nape of her neck. I tugged at the zipper, felt the warmth of her back through the fabric.

"Now look at me!" She stood before me, grinning. The dress showed off her slender waist, her graceful arms, her throat. Red dress, white skin, large, luminous eyes, and brilliant, fragile loveliness. I stared at her amazed, somehow embarrassed and, not for the first time, humbled by her.

"That is a dress for the night," I said. "Your concert is in the afternoon."

"It doesn't matter. I'm the soloist."

"You are too young."

"I want this." Simply.

"I will talk to your father."

She smiled. I realized too late that Tian would let her have what she wanted. "I'll get this little jacket to cover up when I'm not on stage. But I have to have a sleeveless dress, because otherwise I can't move my arms when I play! Call Baba and ask him—he'll say the same thing."

She wanted a few alterations made. I watched her talking with the saleswoman and wondered where she had learned so much about clothes. We rode the subway back to Brooklyn, Anna miserable, Ruth exhilarated. I sat between them. I thought about what would be easiest to make for dinner that night, since we had lost several hours by shopping. Perhaps I would make fried rice, Anna's favorite, since Ruth and Tian in their excitement would scarcely notice what they ate. In the two months since Ruth had won the contest, Tian had been lighthearted, focused, even happy. With only a few weeks to go, he was too agitated to sleep at night. I smiled, thinking of him. But now and then I found myself remembering the sight of my daughter in that dress. I forced the vision away. I did not yet know that in a few weeks it would become a sight I could never forget: my daughter in her scarlet dress, glowing on the stage. Ruth in her red gown in front of the black and white orchestra.

At the first notes of the accompaniment, she lifted up Tian's instrument with a severe, adult authority. She had come of age. Somehow, beneath our eyes, she had grown into herself. I sat in the audience watching her as she began to play. She repeated the theme of the orchestra and drew all of us into the vivid, shining center of the first movement. There was no anger there, none of Tian's bitterness, but youth, sweet youth, drawn from her father's old instrument. The music flowed around us, soothed us and excited us, pulled us away, far away, from ourselves. I remembered the last time I had seen my mother, standing in the airport, waving goodbye to me, framed by the window of the plane. I remembered the city, mysterious and huge as I had first known it, in the blue of evening, with the lit gold windows beckoning from its rooms, the shouts and honks of a million people floating up the avenue. Then I felt Tian shift in his chair and I looked over at him. He sat listening as if to a beloved voice, indelible and persisting over time. He did not wipe away the tears but sat with both hands gripping the arms of his chair, unable to take his tortured, joyful eyes away from the stage.

AT the reception, we discovered we were once again important. Several faculty members from the music school came up to speak to me, including Professor Lydia Borgmann. She had grown coarser in face and body; her hair was streaked with gray.

"Congratulations, Min! She did an absolutely *won*derful job."

"Thank you."

"And you! You look so young! You know, Min, we all used to be so worried about you. He was so gloomy and *fierce*. We thought he might be keeping you locked up, away from us and away from the outside world. Like a little international bride! But no, it turns out you were raising these *mar*velous children." I could see smile lines around her eyes, cutting deep into the papery skin. The memory of how they had shut him out was a burden that she had chosen not to share.

I looked over her shoulder for Ruth and Anna. Anna stood near the corridor in her jumper and blouse, an awkward, growing schoolgirl. She seemed to be edging around the corner toward the coatrack. Ruth and Tian stood deep in conversation with Tian's old dean, Dr. Spaeth, who had made a rare post-performance appearance. I had somehow overlooked him in the audience. I recognized him by his thick mustache, graying now. Tian stood slightly forward, as if protecting Ruth.

Later, we went out for a celebratory dinner. I had chosen the restaurant myself, an Italian place I had often passed on the way from the subway station to a bakery in Chinatown. I had always wanted to have a family dinner there.

We rarely ate away from home. Now I felt glad I had thought of this opportunity. I savored the details I had noticed from the window: the votive candles glowing in little red glasses; checkered tableclothes; wine and sauces. I ordered a glass of wine for myself and one for

Tian, which he would hardly touch. Anna placed her wool jacket carefully on the back of her chair and sat upright, uncomfortable, facing the wall. But Ruth hung her overcoat in the coatrack. She sat down where she could see everything, and unfolded her napkin, daintily, slowly.

No one spoke until we had received our appetizers. Then Ruth said, "Dr. Spaeth said the decision was unanimous. He said I had a rare talent and a great deal of musicality for someone my age."

Tian stabbed his fork into an olive.

Finally I said, "That is good."

"Dr. Spaeth said I could easily get a scholarship to the music school. He said I am a natural performer. He said I had the temperament for it."

She spoke on, her voice excited and pleased. I began to understand. Spaeth had offered to take her on as his own student.

She fixed bright eyes upon her father. "Daddy, can I go?"

We sat quite still for a minute—Anna looked at her plate. Ruth's lips were slightly parted. Tian set down his fork.

"No."

"But Baba—"

"No arguments."

She did not move, but the rich coloring dropped away from her cheeks, and I recalled the way she had looked years earlier, in her brief awkward stage, when the bones of her face had stood out with an almost painful sharpness.

"Why don't we talk about this later?" I suggested, in Chinese.

Ruth nodded, once, stared at her plate. A minute later she got up to use the bathroom. Tian turned to me. "Let me handle this," he said. "She is going to stay with us." He said that he would not allow it—would not allow them to claim they had discovered her, to get their hands on her. They only wanted to exploit her. She would be home-coached, her career managed carefully, by him.

I stared at our table's flickering candle.

He seized my arm. I could feel each finger press into my flesh. "This is how it has to be."

"This—"

From the other side of the table, Anna suddenly spoke, shrill and shaky. "Let her leave! Let her leave! Can't you tell she doesn't want to stay? If you don't let her leave, she'll hate you for as long as she lives."

Tian let go of my arm and swivelled his head to fix her under his gaze. The vein in his jaw stood out and stiffened.

Anna wavered but kept her ground, plain in her plain jumper, rigid and defiant. She whispered, "Don't you think about anyone but yourself?"

They were still staring at each other when Ruth returned to the table. She sat down gracefully, self-possessed again. She had taken off her short jacket, and her bare arms glowed white in the candlelight.

"Put on your jacket," Tian ordered.

"I'm not cold."

"Put it on."

She looked at him, her face a mask. "You can't tell me what to do," she said. "Not now, and not forever."

Tian stood up. "We're going home." We stood and filed out, Anna looking down, wrapped in her wool coat as if it were a shawl, Tian consumed with anger. Ruth strode next to me behind them, her coat draped over one bare white arm. The color had come back into her face and her bright, wide mouth; her resolute, black eyes seemed dangerously still.

She was glittering and silent while we hailed a cab, as

we had planned—this had been my own sad idea, special for the occasion, so much more convenient, and even reasonable with all four of us taking it. Tian sat in front with the driver. He did not once turn to look at us. I sat straight in the back seat, my hands aching from being folded so rigidly in my lap. This question of Ruth's leaving us, once asked, could never be retracted. I knew that someday she would do this. What would become of us? The performance, so innocently looked forward to, had sent our family hurtling in a direction I could not navigate. The gray and white evening surrounded our car, and we seemed to coast the half-mile to Brooklyn in an absolute silence.

Our apartment door had barely closed behind us when she whirled on him, her red lips pursed as if she were about to spit on his face.

"Let me go! You have to let me go!"

Tian took her roughly by the arm and pulled her into the living room.

"You're staying here."

"Let go of my arm! You're hurting me!"

"You are not leaving this house as long as you are still a child. Do you hear me?"

"I'm not a child!"

"You're my daughter and I'm your father!"

When Ruth emerged from the living room a minute later she had wiped her eyes dry with her sleeve, and except for their red rims, her face was pale and creamy. She walked into her bedroom, her muscles stiff after the long day. She climbed the ladder into the upper bunk. There she stayed, and would not answer questions. She would not speak to me and she pretended not to hear Anna asking her if it was all right to come in.

I sat up in the kitchen until after midnight. In our room I could hear Tian's footsteps, treading in circles for what seemed like more than an hour. The old floor creaked; the footsteps circled. I did not want to face him, to comfort him, or to let him speak about how much he hated the people from the music school. I thought of the concert, of his tortured face, tilted up toward the stage, Ruth's pained surprise in the restaurant, her transformation and resentment. Toward one o'clock, the footsteps stopped. I put down the newspaper and tiptoed toward the room. My heart sank when I saw the bar of yellow light under the door. I opened it.

Tian sat in bed, in his pajamas, waiting for me. The light threw shadows over his face and his eyes, enormous, burned into mine.

"Still awake?" My pleasantry fooled no one. I turned to face the closet. I slid my feet from their shoes, unbuttoned my shirt. I remembered my clip earrings—my lobes were numb—and had just slid them off when I heard a click and the room went dark. Tian had turned out the light. He got out of the bed and walked slowly over to me, stood directly behind me. I held still for a few fierce seconds.

I did not want him to touch me. His breath, heavy with garlic from the restaurant meal, struck my cheek. I did not turn around. I pulled on my pajama pants, buttoned my top. After a long moment, Tian turned and got back into bed.

EACH morning brings an opportunity for surprise. Perhaps we never feel this as clearly as we do when we first come into our own power. Watching Ruth, I remembered my courage in the moment, so long ago, when I had seized Tian's hat in my hands. Perhaps it was the scarlet dress, the nourishment of performance and applause. I only know that sometime around then, in her fifteenth year, Ruth began to sense a world outside our house, a world quivering with power and promise. In those warm, spring evenings she stood out on the fire escape, head high, breathing in its scent.

She stayed in public school with Anna, and continued after Anna left for college. She kept practicing with Tian. But she had developed a sudden and brilliant genius for upsetting him. So many years of pleasing him had given her this ability. With me she remained obedient. I prided myself on this, until I recognized it as an emblem of indifference. My pale love would never interest her. Tian was her true opponent, and I was only a moth that fluttered around the brilliant bulb of her rebellion.

Her energy grew so high that she could not sleep, and she returned to her childhood habit of climbing out of bed and wandering through the house. Or she stayed in bed but read with her flashlight, tapping out rhythms on the iron bedstead. One night I got up to use the bathroom. On my return, I saw a straight, slender shadow at the window. She stood at the living room window in her pajamas, looking out at the night.

"Are you all right?" I asked.

To my gratitude and surprise, she made room for me beside her. There was little to see. The row of brownstones stood patiently, their brick fronts shadowed. A gray cat slipped out from under a car and stretched, casting its neat, arched shadow on the pale sidewalk.

Watching the street, Ruth whispered, "Mom. Did you ever want to go somewhere else?"

She had an unsettling gentleness and sympathy that surfaced occasionally when we were alone. At such moments, I felt guilty that I had not tried to work with this softness, to help her gain some control over the more difficult side of her nature. I found it impossible to lie to her. "Sometimes," I said. "Sometimes I do."

"If you could go anywhere in the world, where would you go?"

The words slipped from my mouth. "I want to go to Taiwan." It was true. Years had passed since I had let myself remember how much I wanted to leave New York. I yearned to smell the wetness of tropical rain, to leave the city and climb into the forest, to see the mountains, the rich green trees, the lush rotting earth. My mother's ashes lay in that land, and I believed her soul would welcome all of us, would help keep all of us together.

"I didn't know you liked Taiwan."

I thought about this. "I did," I said. "A lot." As I spoke, I hated the simple English words that came out of my mouth. There was so much I wanted to say to her. I wanted to say that no, I hadn't loved Taiwan when I was there, but that now the thought of it made me want to weep. I wanted to tell her that when you stay in one place long enough, it becomes a part of you whether you want it to or not. But I did not own those words.

Ruth seemed to understand what I wanted to say. "Maybe you will be able to go back sometime," she said.

The bedroom door creaked open and Tian came out. He whispered loudly, "Go to bed!"

I put a hand on Ruth's shoulder. I had planned to give her a little push, to help Tian, but I realized that I did not want to help him, that I wanted to hold onto her. She was so gentle that night, and kind. Ruth moved only after several seconds, languidly, drifting toward her room. Tian walked with her, through the kitchen, and stood sternly next to her door as she entered. I heard the creak of the top bunk as she climbed into it. Anna had vacated the bottom bunk when she had left for school, but Ruth did not wish to move; she wanted her privacy.

Tian accused me later of encouraging her disobedience. "You don't care!" he shouted, then tried to speak more gently: "You don't understand, perhaps, what an important time this is for her. You let her do whatever she wants!" Despite his efforts, his voice grew thick with anger. "It's as if you think that letting her have her way is more important than her music."

He spoke the truth, and since he spent his evening hours at the restaurant, the blame for her wildness must rightly fall on me. I let her stay late at school and eat dinner with her friends; I saw no great harm in buying her a guitar for her birthday, even if it meant I had encouraged her to play an instrument that forced her hands into an incorrect position. I did not set a curfew as long as she returned before her father came home. I had never censored Anna's words or actions, and so I didn't think it right to argue with her younger sister. Ruth would not have stood for it, I suspected. I had no control over what she did. She spoke often of being independent—"I need my independence! I'm American, not Chinese!"—and I came to believe that the only way to keep her with us involved this leniency, bartering permissiveness for her continued presence. Even now, I don't think Tian or I could have changed her ways by working differently or together. The wilfulness, the intense desires, ran in her blood.

She had a passion for wandering that grew the more her father tried to keep her home. I don't know how he discovered she wasn't taking the city bus to school in the mornings. I believe she must have told him. She had a way of seeming ignorant of all consequences. Somehow he discovered that Ruth had been catching rides to school with the older brother of a friend. The quarrel rose suddenly out of a quiet dinner conversation.

Hunger

"*Who* is giving you these rides?"

"Sheila's brother," Ruth replied. She twirled the joint of a chicken wing and slipped the piece into her mouth. She looked tired, but not afraid of her father. I stared at her mouth, which closed around the end of the chicken bone; I noticed her puffy lips, the shadows under her eyes, and I knew that Tian had seen all of this.

"Let me walk to school with you." The words slipped out of me.

She looked at me as if she had never seen me before and, in a delicate dismissal, rolled her eyes.

Tian ignored my statement. "I need to know that you are where you are supposed to be!" His chopsticks, laden with cauliflower, wavered, and the food dropped back onto his plate. Ruth chewed dreamily, absorbed. She balanced her rice bowl in slender fingers and reached out for a few more leaves of bok choy.

She left the dinner table while Tian and I were peeling our oranges. My hands trembled. Did my opinion mean so little to him?

I said, "You shouldn't be so harsh with her. Don't worry about her and she'll give you less cause for worry."

"She's trying to get away with too much," he said harshly, in English. He stood up, and left the kitchen, his unfinished fruit on the table. For a moment his words echoed. I had thought he was going to say, "She's trying to get away."

I finished my orange. I stood up and cleared away our rice bowls, chopsticks, and serving bowls, but the dishes chattered as if they were coming alive in my hands. From the hallway came the sound of slow, deliberate footsteps, the groan of the floorboards. Someone moving heavy furniture.

"What is it?" I called. The dragging sound grew louder. Then Tian's armchair, turned sideways, entered the kitchen, with Tian behind it. He had pushed and dragged it from the living room.

"What are you doing?" I asked.

He did not answer me but settled the chair near the girls' bedroom door. Then he walked out of the kitchen again and returned a minute later, carrying blankets and a pillow.

He planned to sleep in front of the door. He wanted to make certain Ruth stayed in her room.

"You put that back. This is too much." I did not recognize my voice.

He slowly turned to me. His voice was low and terse. "I want to know where my daughters are. I want to make sure that my daughter stays in bed at night, as I have told her to."

I tried to speak. Then I tried again. My words came out then, first a whisper. "You're being unreasonable."

Tian looked up at me. His eyes were bleak, a stranger's eyes. "You keep out of this," he said. "This has nothing to do with you."

"What do you mean by that?"

"I mean exactly what I said!"

I felt my toes push into the floor, as if my density had multiplied. I felt myself grow taller, tower over him. My head had become suddenly enormous, my lungs cavernous. I heard my breathing hiss and lash.

"Is that what you think?" I asked him, my voice crackling and cold. "Perhaps you're right. It has nothing to do with me. Nothing has to do with me. She's your daughter, isn't she? She was always yours. You taught her what was important! Now you live with the results."

We stood back, amazed at the finality in those words.

My voice had laid a welt on the air, like the trail of a whip.

That night he slept in the chair next to the door. I did not speak to him when he came to change into his pajamas or the next morning, when he put them away.

This began our period of silence, thick and strangely comforting to me, like an insulated wall. When Anna came home from college the day before Thanksgiving, she noticed our rift immediately.

"What about Baba?" she asked that night. Tian was working late, and I had cleared away the dinner dishes without setting out his plate and bowl.

"Baba is fine."

"No! No, he isn't fine. Don't be angry with him," she begged.

She could not understand—our silence was a kind of resting place, a truce. We had said enough to last quite a while. We were giving each other, for a time, the right to leave each other alone.

It ended a few weeks later. I woke up to go to the bathroom and found him in his chair, wrapped in a striped sheet and cotton blanket. A cold breeze came from the window, and I walked over to close it. He roused himself and squinted at me. "I'm all right," he said. "Go back to bed."

So our silence passed, but from then on we both understood that I would not challenge him again. I had left the two of them; I was no longer responsible for them. For a few weeks he continued to sleep in the chair. Ruth said nothing about it, but during those weeks she stayed in bed all night. One day as I emptied out her wastebasket I leaped back in fright as two heavy metal cylinders thumped out and rolled across the floor. They were the heavy-duty batteries from her flashlight.

ANNA had not gone far away. She enrolled at Columbia, on a full scholarship for bright and needy students. College changed her; she discovered a place where she could relax. She found friends at school; she seemed happy there. But every other weekend she took the subway home, and when she opened the door there was still that watchfulness about her. She would sit at the kitchen table with me, her eyes darting over my shoulder and around the apartment to see if anything had changed.

I missed her terribly. Late afternoons and evenings, with Ruth spending time with friends from school, were the most difficult. It was at such times that Anna and I had kept each other company. But now things were as quiet as snowfall. I would sit and remember her as a child: I remembered again and again the way I had turned to face the wall when she was born. I would remind myself of the many years we had shared together. I missed her but I did not want to interrupt this precious new life she had made.

One night when Tian was at the restaurant, Anna suddenly called home.

"How is school?" I asked. "Is there a problem? Do you need anything?"

"No. I just—I had a weird dream, that's all, and I thought I'd call you."

I understood what she was trying to say. "We're fine at home," I said. "Don't worry about us."

"Do you ever have premonitions?"

"What is that?"

"A thought that comes true."

I remembered my premonition in the restaurant, the day I had given Tian his hat. I was not surprised to learn that Anna had similar moments. But for some reason, perhaps the secret fickleness that visits a mother's love, I did not feel compelled to reveal my thoughts to Anna. Her sympathy, unlike Ruth's, did not arouse my confidence. I don't know why this was true, but it was a fact: I did not share with Anna the story of the moment when I had held Tian's hat in my hand and realized what my future would be. "Yes," I said politely. "I do. But we are okay, Anna."

"I know. I just wanted to call home for some reason. How is everything at home?"

"Everything is okay," I told her. "How are your classes?"

She chattered on this topic for several minutes. Away from Tian and me, she seemed to have turned even more resolutely to those issues that had, at home, been cast aside: she studied the Chinese language, history, literature. She could recite the long line of dynasties as well as I had ever been taught to do. She had even begun to read in translation modern Chinese authors whom I had never bothered to look at. She developed a passionate interest in China's warlord era, and the role internal factions and coalitions had played in the events that followed the Japanese invasion. I could not understand this. Was she not interested in the present, or the future?

She asked, "Do you think that Baba would participate in an oral history project?"

"What is an oral history?"

"I would tape and transcribe a series of interviews in which he described his childhood and the way he remembers the events of that time."

I heard a touching new confidence in her voice. At school she had also discovered the seductive and naive idea that there lay some hope of healing in mining the past, in digging it out and laying it down before others. She had lost her whine, had grown self-possessed, attractive. But through her intellect and sophistication I could still detect—in a certain eagerness, a catch of breath—the yearning that had always tortured her.

"You can ask him," I said, "but he might be angry. He doesn't like to talk."

"Maybe talking about it will make him feel better," she suggested.

"Maybe." After we hung up, I wondered whether I had been too discouraging. Perhaps Anna might persuade Tian to tell his story if she pointed out that it was for a school project? But I knew better. He had made a bargain with himself.

He had not told this story to me when we were young and hopeful, and in love, and there was no way he would tell it now. The shadow of his past had covered him, and he could no longer see us. Oh, he and I kept up our routines, but it was as if his heart had relocated elsewhere. And I admit it. I was glad of it. Long ago he had begun to disappoint me. I had grown to disappoint myself. I did not want to face this, and I knew there was no point in our discussing the dissolution of Tian's dreams. There also remained the matter of Ruth; I was too proud to fight with him over Ruth. Most of all I could not face the fact that I had allowed my daughter to be subjected to her father—to his unremitting desires, his stubborn memories, his fury and personal disappointment. But I sometimes wonder if I could ever have protected Ruth, ever made a difference? Perhaps the map of our lives in this house had been drawn from the moment I first set my eyes on Tian, or tried to speak to him, or looked down at his worn hat and read his name.

Hunger

ONLY once did he ask for my advice. This happened during the fall of Ruth's junior year. I heard a quarrel, then a silence, and their footsteps, measured and formal, approaching the kitchen. I had been straightening the upper cabinets. I climbed off the stepstool.

"Let's ask Mom. We're asking Mom," I heard Tian's voice in the foyer, close. The stepstool clattered over as I turned, surprised and inexplicably apprehensive at this decision. I flushed as I bent to pick it up. They burst into the kitchen.

"We have decided to ask you," Tian announced. He stood with Ruth behind him, his hands clenched.

"What is it?" I asked. I set the chair aside and turned to face them.

"She wants to go to a dance," Tian said. He stopped and waited for my reaction.

"A dance is okay," I said. "Do you have a ride?"

"I have a ride," Ruth announced.

"Okay," I said, bewildered.

"She says okay," Ruth mimicked me.

"Then go!" Tian shouted. "You go! I'll withdraw you from the competition!"

I turned to stare at him.

"Go ahead," Ruth replied. She stood absolutely still, one slim hip cocked, so certain of her beauty and of the sensual precociousness with which she guarded her privacy. She had not blinked at Tian's decision but remained poised gracefully on her long legs, her black head tilted away from her father, toward the window. She was underweight, her slitted eyes black, her face bleached bone. I could not take my eyes from the dark, thumb-sized callous on her pale throat, under her left jaw, where a violin will leave its mark on the person who is faithful to it.

Tian turned to me with an air of expectation. I understood that there was something irrelevant in his choosing me for this arbitration. He could not even see me, and I had the sensation I had had so many times in our marriage, but never as much as in recent years, that I was looking at the face of a stranger. The kitchen lamp brought out each line of his face—the hollows underneath his eyes, the lines around his mouth. I could see the outline of his skull.

"This dance," he said to me, lips set close together, "is the night before the competition. *The night before.*"

Ruth's black head swiveled and she locked her father in her obsidian gaze. It was as if a fishing line had suddenly been tightened between the two of them, although who was the fisher and who the fish I wasn't certain. I took a deep breath, tried to stay calm.

"Tell your mother what you told me!"

She looked at me through somber, treacherous eyes. She took her time, and when she spoke, her voice was chilling and quiet. "I don't like playing the violin," she said. "In fact, I never liked it. I hate it, as a matter of fact."

I noticed sudden dark patches of sweat under Tian's arms and great drops clinging to his forehead. I took a breath, and it hurt my chest, as if a hook had caught me there.

"I don't see why she can't do both, if she gets home in time," I told Tian in Chinese. This banal and hopeful statement slid from my mouth as if encased in a bubble and hung quivering in the air between us.

After one stunned moment, they relaxed. Their eyes met, and I knew that I had been lured and caught by them, and for their purposes.

Then Tian motioned with his chin that the arbitration had ended. She turned to him, her long limbs falling into obedience. I understood that I had been consulted not to give advice or even to mediate the conflict but to play a minor role in their drama: to remind them of their own ties to each other. They had found the necessary third party that would keep them, for the moment, moving on. Without a word, they walked out of the kitchen, Ruth drifting ahead and Tian following, watchful and proprietary. I felt foolish then for thinking that I could have any part of this. I reminded myself that I had forfeited my right to interfere. But I was still angry at both of them, so angry that my vision blurred and I felt so dizzy I had to stop cleaning. I was afraid of having some kind of accident with the stepstool.

Two nights later, the night of the school dance, I woke up suddenly with a strong feeling that something had gone wrong. It was so late that the traffic sounds had died away. I slid out of bed, tiptoed through the living room and the foyer, into the kitchen. No Ruth. Her bedroom door was closed. For some reason I went to the kitchen window. The air felt chilly, as if the window had been recently opened. I felt, rather than heard, a movement; looking up, I saw the shadow of Ruth's narrow foot disappear off the top rung of the fire escape and over the edge of the roof. She moved carefully, so carefully that I could hardly hear her footsteps above my head. I stood and wondered what I should do. Outside, below, the valley of backyards lay buried in a tangle of half-grown trees and laundry lines and old couches, dark.

As children, the girls had discovered a trick of jiggling the kitchen window from the outside in such a way as to loosen the lock — a delicate business. So I knew she would be able to slip back in without disturbing our bedroom's end of the house. Did Tian know she had been sneaking out? Was that why he had begun the business with the chair? When I thought of him, I felt my pulse thump with resentment. I decided to let things go and I went back to bed.

But I dreamed Ruth cast a spell upon the house, which shrunk down small enough to fit into her bag. She did not take me along with her. She strode away in the middle of the night, and I lay unable to move in my bed, in the middle of the driveway, exposed under a gleaming spiderweb of stars.

I woke suddenly, startled awake by some small sound. I lay there, half asleep and frightened, thinking that perhaps it had been nothing at all, but after a while I heard again a tiny crackling noise. It was the sound of ice cubes being shaken in the kitchen. I slid out of bed, thankful for Tian's snoring, because I had a feeling he would not want to see this. Near the door to my room I heard something else that made me pause — a human sound, like a quick intake of breath.

I listened silently at my door. I heard her walking from the kitchen, heels light on the floor. Then some murmuring, closer by, a barely stifled chuckle. Why was it that at that sound, the stifled laugh of a boy, I knew she had stifled it with her own hands? And why, in the silences and muffled sounds, could I imagine each gesture, each caress, that I knew was taking place in her small bedroom? I crept back to our bed and lay back down.

Tian spoke suddenly from the dark. "What is it?" he asked. He sounded exhausted. He had returned from the restaurant, as usual, at eleven o'clock.

"Nothing," I said. "Just go back to sleep."

I DID not interfere. I did not ask Tian what he knew. But I watched the fights take on a desperate intensity. Even after Ruth won the competition, they continued. Seldom a moment passed when both were at home and awake that they were not lost in some kind of fury. Each demand, each refusal and retort, would escalate their mutual rage.

It was once traditional in Chinese culture for a daughter to leave the house of her birth and move in with her husband's family. For this reason, Chinese mothers must steel themselves to part with their daughters. In the U.S., I knew, this parting was not necessary; for example, our neighbor, Mrs. Lici, spent every Sunday with her daughter Rozanna. But that would not be true of Ruth; I knew she would someday leave. Tian refused to acknowledge this; he fought and struggled against the thought, but it continued to beat against his stubborn resistance, an inexorable tide coming in against a shore of stone.

The two of them kept to their rituals. On Monday evenings, as she practiced, Tian shouted, pounding his fist on the piano, thudding his feet against the floor, writhing in his chair as if he were chained in it. I watched, my vision blurring as if my eyes were being damaged from looking at the sun.

One night, a week before she was scheduled to perform, everything grew somehow worse, far worse than it had ever been. I stayed in my room. Every half-hour or so my own fear propelled me into the kitchen, where they fought. "It's too late," I would say. "Go to sleep." Or "The neighbors will hear you." But they behaved as if I did not exist. Their voices split and cracked, rising like a storm wind, unbearable in the sheer force of emotion. It was a force you could see shapes in, colors like black-purple and scarlet and venomous yellow-green.

"You will stay in this house!" "I am not staying!" "You will obey me and go to sleep!" "You can't keep me from leaving!" "You will stay in this house and practice!" "I hate you, I hate you!" "You're going to kill me! You'll make me die!" This made her cry, her sobbing higher and higher, but neither of them acknowledged her tears.

Finally I heard her say, "I'm quitting! I'm never going

to pick up a violin again for as long as I live."

And without a pause, he cried, "Then I don't want you! You are not my daughter! You are nothing!"

His words flew into a gulf of silence. Finally she replied, sounding thin and faraway. "Well, that's it," she said.

An hour of relative peace went by. Sometime later, Tian came into our room and shut the door. He stumbled over to the bed and sat on the edge, weeping. I sat in my chair, pretending to read, unable to speak. Minutes passed; I thought he would not acknowledge me, but then finally he said, "I can't make her stay. I can't."

I said nothing.

"Listen to me!" he cried. "She's leaving, I'm telling you! She's packing her things."

The truth in his voice jarred me to action. I ran out, through the dark living room, the foyer, the kitchen.

The lights in the bedroom were on. The pink bed-spreads threw a violent glow against the walls. Ruth stood in the middle of the room, taking out clothes from the chest of drawers and packing them into my old carpetbag. She packed quickly and silently, closing each drawer after she opened it, folding each piece of clothing with precise ges-tures. She had pulled her hair into a neat ponytail. After a long moment, I became aware that Tian had followed me. I turned to look at him, but the expression on his face was so terrible I had to look away. He simply stood and watched. I feared for a moment that one of them might break down, might crack. What would happen then? But they did not. When she had finished, she shouldered the half-full bag, picked up her guitar case, and walked out of the room. Tian stayed where he was; he stood in the door, immobi-lized and weak, as if watching a scene he had long dreaded, or dreamed about, or foreseen, long ago.

I followed her out the door and down the stairs.

HUNGER

"Please," I said. "Please stay. You're not old enough." At the bottom of the stairs, I reached out for her arm. She turned and faced me.

"Just leave me be," she said. I heard no anger in her voice, only weariness. I let my hand fall to my side.

"One minute," I said. "Please stay here for a minute." I hurried back up the stairs, through the open door, and to the place where I had hidden the envelope that held my store of cash. Seventeen fifty-dollar bills, one for each year of her life. I snatched it out and hurried back down the stairs.

She stood waiting at the door, suddenly obedient under the weary entrance light. Her lashes cast shadows over her high cheekbones. I stood there with my daughter at the shabby door of our building, with the apartment dark and heavy over us, and for what did not seem like a very long few minutes I looked into her face. And I found, for a moment, a look of myself about the eyes, in the way she smiled at me gently, mouth closed. I had not felt like an adequate mother to her, and she had never wanted me. But I was her mother now, at this moment of departure. I understood that although I had been a poor enough mother to her, it was all the same in the end. Everything I had ever done against or for Ruth had been moving toward this point of leaving. I knew this and she knew it also. She waited, looking carefully down while I struggled with my tears. She had for some reason forgiven me.

"Here," I said. "Please. And be careful. And please come home, Ruyu, come home."

She took the money, folded it, and slid it into her pocket.

"Thank you, Mother," she said. Then she walked to the door, opened it, and stepped outside.

MANY YEARS AGO, WHEN I LIVED IN TAIPEI with my parents, we were visited by a thief. Like many island buildings of that time, our house had been designed after a Japanese dwelling, with light wood screens and fragile walls. The burglar entered easily, smashing his hand through the window and reaching in to unlock the door.

He ignored my father's cheap radio. Through some uncanny instinct, he found almost every object that my parents had preserved from their lives on the mainland. The figured silk my mother had brought from Shanghai. One translucent and thin-edged rice bowl from my father's household. A string of carmine prayer beads that had been a present from my older aunt.

The thief behaved well, for a criminal—he did not break or spill anything, and he locked the door when he had finished, as if to preserve what he had left behind. If it had not been for that hole in the window, we might have returned from the wedding and gone to sleep without noticing the change. But we saw the hole, and we did not sleep. My mother stayed awake for hours. She attempted to compile a list of every item that had disappeared. She went through each of our small rooms, opening boxes, searching shelves. But she could make no easy inventory of such loss. For weeks afterward, she would reach for something and find it missing, and she would weep the helpless tears of one whose life has slid through aging hands. That year my father fell ill, and my mother and I were faced with a much more difficult loss.

Years later, after Ruth walked out of our house, I found myself remembering the aftermath of this strange robbery that had taken place so long ago and far away. We found ourselves in a similar process—first, a telephone interview with the police. Tian called them the morning after she left, when he had reached the limit of his ability to cope with his own helplessness. He fixed on the possibility that the police would find her. But I knew she did not wish to be found. In the end, I was correct. The officer listened to my numb remarks, Tian's fixed, dull insistence that they "do something," Anna's puzzled and unhelpful replies to his indifferent questions. Which high school did Ruth attend? Might there be a teacher or counselor who would know of her plans? Had she mentioned the names of any friends she might be staying with? But time went by, with no sign that she had contacted anyone, as if she had vanished from the earth.

Later I would be writing a letter or taking a bath. I would reach for some household object and my hand would close on an empty space. A pair of scissors, a tube of skin cream. She had put these things in her bag. I would give way to a shameful, silent gushing of tears, as my own mother had years earlier when she had reached for a stolen item and found it missing; I cried sometimes for hours if there was no one at home and nothing to stop me. I wept for Ruth, and for my parents, for Anna and for Tian. Most of all I wept for myself, in a panic that this powder-brush might be the final item I would ever miss, and then she truly would be gone.

The officer advised Anna to stay near her dormitory for several days, on the chance that Ruth might seek her out there. But I knew, and Anna knew, that Ruth would not have flown to family, would not have considered her sister a refuge. After a week, when this knowledge had been confirmed, Anna called to ask if I wanted her at home.

"I don't want to take you away from school," I said.

"It would be easier if you would let me help."

"I'm fine."

"Easier for me," she said.

"I'll be okay."

"All right." When had Anna grown up, developed the ability to offer help and to accept the refusal of this offer? It was I who was not ready to accept comfort.

She began to visit more frequently, and although we still didn't talk much, we began to take a grudging pleasure in our time together. One evening on spring break, while watching a television show of amateur rock and roll bands, she jumped up in a kind of terror over the shadowy figure of a bass guitarist. She called me into the room, and when the whole band flickered back on the screen I saw that the guitarist did look very much like Ruth—although taller, thinner, gaunter-faced. "It's not her," I said. "I know. But I wanted someone else to see. I'm sorry." "That's all right." Then the camera slid away.

I could still picture Ruth vividly—not the scarlet mouth and angry eyes of the last few years, but as she had been in earlier times. I could smell and feel her baby breath on my throat. I envisioned her at twelve, performing for me in the kitchen, grown suddenly thin and tall. She was finishing the final movement of the Mendelssohn concerto, whipping her bow off her strings in a triumphant gesture. Over and over I remembered one sunny afternoon at the park when she was three years old. I had reached for her dress when she had leaped out of my lap to follow a pigeon as it took flight. The dress, a yellow print, had torn; I remembered the sound and shape of the tear. I had reached for her and her dress had torn. I had been angry, I had scolded her that day.

After seventeen years with her, I had grown accustomed to the sounds my daughter made around the house: the precise thump of her narrow heels against the wooden floors; the laugh that in recent years she had reserved for conversations on the phone; the rich, almost carelessly perfect trills and runs that escaped from the practice room. Even her arguments with Tian could be identified by a certain rhythm: a duet of high and low voices, rising to a wounded cry, then a silence during which I heard the faint, surrounding hints of traffic. After she left, the silence in the house grew; it took on weight and presence; nothing could break it. It could scarcely be borne.

A MONTH to the day after she left—a Monday evening—Tian and I were watching television when he suddenly flattened against his chair and took a dragging, hollow breath. I leaned over him. His face went gray; his eyes, wide open, seemed to stiffen like wax.

"Tian!" I cried. Slowly, his eyes cleared. I had called him back. He had been returned to himself and me, for a brief time, at least.

Later that night, the doctors told me that his heart would not recover. Damage had been done; the muscle beat unsteadily and could not send out enough blood. Tian lay in his hospital bed, gaunt and silent. He was conscious, but he refused to answer Anna when she rushed into the room, still clutching the change from her subway token, and said over and over, "Baba." He lay listening to the weak and seizing sounds of his own blood. Perhaps he was preparing himself for what he must have known would happen next.

At the end of visiting hours I sent Anna back to the apartment, but I found myself unable to leave. The nurses held a whispered conversation and decided to let me stay. Tian did not thank me or say he wanted me there, but when I walked into the room after taking Anna to the elevator, he opened his eyes and looked at me.

Twenty-one years, and I had never admitted my disappointment with him. I had not complained about a lack of money or time together. I had taken what he brought home and made it into our daily lives. In truth, how selfish I had been. If I had shown my anger—would that not have eased his burden of shame, released him from some responsibility for our unhappiness? How my disappointment must have weighed on him, silently reproaching. I wished that I had done something to make it easier. Sitting at his hospital bed, I felt an almost overpowering need to tell him that my desires had been nothing, that I had been a petty, cowardly woman. But after a moment I began to think that I would not, after all, begin this conversation. I could have done nothing to appease him. I could never have made up for what he had lost for himself. Unburdening myself would have been inappropriate, even selfish. Tian was short of breath, and we had talked less and less, it seemed, as time had passed.

The hallway lights dimmed and the hospital grew hushed and dark. We had been sitting in the dark for almost an hour when Tian began to speak.

He whispered, "I was at a coffeehouse in Taipei. I saw a copy of an American news magazine, a photograph of the young Israeli violinist, performing at the New York Philharmonic. Then I knew I had to go to New York. If I could get to New York, I would be able to succeed."

"You did well," I said.

His hand flickered on the dim counterpane to wave away what I had said.

"You lived an honest life," I said.

"It was never my desire to live an honest life."

He closed his eyes. For several minutes he lay there, and then he said without opening his eyes, "I didn't think about the hardships and sacrifices I was making, but of what was going to be. Even after getting fired, I didn't think about my job. That restaurant. But I focused on what was going to be. Whenever I looked at—Anna's sister." He would not say her name. "Whenever I looked at her, I saw the violinist that she might be. I saw past her poor behavior, her disobedience, her laziness, and I could see it—brilliance, like a star."

He stopped. I turned my head, unable to watch him try to hide his tears.

After almost half an hour, he said, "When I first moved here, before I even met you, I used to listen to the radio all night. I would look out the window at the lights across the river and pretend that they were stars.

"I kept thinking of the future. But I didn't understand. The future was already there. The future lay around me all those years. The conservatory would never have given me tenure. Then the restaurant. And Ruth. One good look, and it would have been clear to any fool that all that hoping was a waste."

"It's not a waste."

"Too lazy to rosin her bow. Movie-star pictures under her bed. And the things she did. I know what she did. She was like a little whore."

I said, "You were good to me. And good to Anna. You worked hard for me and Anna."

His fierce eyes were fixed on the ceiling. "That is not important."

Toward morning he woke from a sound sleep and shifted on the bed, as if he were getting out of it. His eyes, wide open, implacable, traced the distance between the bed and the closed door, settling on the door, the gray line of light underneath.

"Tian," I said. Then, "Tian, where are you going?"

He took two dragging breaths. Then he placed both hands on his chest and died.

Some Chinese make their fortunes in America. Tian

and I were not among them. Perhaps we lacked the forgetfulness that is essential to moving on. I know where Tian has gone in death. He has made his way west, retraced the route he so many years earlier traveled by bus, when he had just arrived in this country and set off to make his fortune in New York. Now he would be returning, across the width of this continent, back to San Francisco. He would not stop for a moment there in that city on the edge of the earth, before plunging over the bright Pacific.

When he reaches the house, he will once again be disappointed. I have seen it in a dream: the shell of the house has been rebuilt and another home erected in its courtyard, to save space in the new and growing country. But on some violet evenings, when the light of late summer infuses each corner and angle with light, it might be possible to forget that any time has passed, and as dusk gives way to night the moonlight makes familiar shapes, recalling old shadows. I hope this memory can satisfy his ghost—that the sight of these shapes will give him rest, will help him to forget.

MY own story, what there is of it, remains here in this house.

After Tian's death, I went through several years with surprising ease. It was as if I had lost half my weight; like a blade of grass, I blew light and dry through the decisions and planning allotted me. I received help from a few surprising sources. Tian had kept a small benefits package from his years at the music school, of which I was the beneficiary. Da Dao took up a collection at the restaurant. We had kept our own small savings account. Altogether I had enough to make a down payment on our apartment, with Anna reading the papers for me, when the units in the brownstone went up for sale. I had no desire to live anywhere else.

Hunger

I quit working at the restaurant and found a job at a shoe store off Atlantic Avenue, close to home, and I stayed there without incident for two years. I discovered, to my surprise, that by listening to and speaking with my daughters I had learned enough English to answer almost all of the customers' questions. As a matter of fact, whole days went by when I did not speak a word of Mandarin, and I might never have needed to if not for occasional phone calls from my mother's sister, phone calls that came less and less frequently with the years, and if Anna had not insisted now and then on using the language with me in order to practice. It was as if I were a member of a dying tribe, and those with whom I cared to communicate were growing fewer and fewer. But who does not experience this as they grow older; who does not find that there is less and less to talk about as the handful of those most precious to them grow fewer and eventually disappear? Haven't we all, as time continues, found that we must be kind to ourselves and listen to our thoughts, because fewer and fewer of those remain who know what is most real to us?

Walking home one October day, the wind whipping dried husks of leaves before my feet, I felt alerted to some new scent that had blown into the air. When I climbed the stairs I noticed old Mrs. Lici standing in her doorway, her bulldog face hovering over the safety chain. She did not speak to me, and I walked past her without a word. I turned the keys in the lock and deadbolt and stepped into the foyer. I took off my gloves and unwrapped my heavy scarf. Then I looked into the living room and saw my lost daughter.

She stood just three yards away from me, dressed all in black, a precise slim shape. She stood still as if she were a deer and camouflaged by the room around her. A deep draft of cold air flowed around us from an open window.

"Ruth," I said. I touched on the word carefully, as if my tongue would burn the roof of my mouth. I walked toward her.

She had grown thinner, almost gaunt, and my first impression was that her coloring and beauty had been worn away. I could see the tendons in her throat, the collarbone standing out over the scoop neckline of her black knit sweater. She looked like a person carved from colorless stone, and as I walked closer I saw that her pale skin was also like stone, faintly weathered around the eyes and the corners of her mouth. But after a minute my vision cleared, as if I had been looking into a pool of water whose ripples had grown still. I could trace the shape of her bones again, the somber, lovely lines of her face.

She said, "You still have the old bunk bed." I listened to the sound of her high voice and the way she shaped her words—with unusual precision and clarity, but lingering on the nouns. Her voice sounded a little rough, like a boy's.

"I'm happy to see you," I said. "I'm happy you came home."

In the silence that followed this remark I moved closer to hug her; she backed away. I patted her arm. She seemed ready to crackle at the touch, as if she were charged with static electricity.

"This isn't my home," she said.

I asked her if she wanted something to drink.

"Do you mind if I smoke?"

"That's okay."

"You hate it, I can tell."

I opened my mouth to argue, but stopped. More than anything, my irritation reminded me we were still not strangers. But I felt more than a little uneasy, making my way through an old minefield in the dark.

She followed me into the kitchen, her footsteps echoing. As we left the foyer, I caught a glimpse of her in the mirror. She walked with an authority of movement that revealed an awareness of her body; I recalled, for a moment, her appearance on the stage. In the jut of her angular hips was something of that confidence, the certitude of a woman who lived without ambiguity, who had been whittled down to essentials. She wore jeans, boots, and a jacket cut of soft, luxurious black leather.

"Would you like something to eat?"

"I'm not hungry."

"A cup of tea? Some milk?"

She looked at me, then turned her gaze across the kitchen counter, pausing at my single tea mug, the rice bowl in the dishrack.

"He's gone, isn't he?"

I told her how.

She took a deep breath. Her expression did not change, and at that moment I realized why she looked so much like Tian. Her eyes were like her father's eyes, dark and lost and unrelenting. Finally she said, "I had a feeling he was gone." She looked at our warped linoleum floor.

"Do you want me to tell you more about it?"

"No."

"Can I get you anything?"

"I don't think so—I'm only in the city for a few hours. I'm on a layover for a flight to France. But I think I'd like to take a shower, if that's all right. I came in all the way from San Francisco."

She had not used a key. She walked to the kitchen window, reached out onto the fire escape, and produced a black duffel bag, which she set on the table. I stood in the door and watched her sort through her things. How could she pack so little for a trip to France? I saw a blouse of silk, a red-bound personal calendar, and several vials and jars of expensive-looking skin creams that she wrapped in a clean t-shirt and carried to the bathroom. She began to close the door but stuck her head out at the last minute and smiled almost nervously. "Be out in a minute!" One slender hand emerged and fluttered goodbye before the door shut firmly behind her.

I heard the water turn on. After a moment, I remembered that Ruth had a way of taking long showers, as if she needed the inexorable feeling of hot water beating against her skin. I knew that it would be not one but forty minutes before she was finished, and retrieving this bit of information about my daughter was like chipping a piece from an enormous stone that I had allowed to harden in the most forbidden corners of my memory. Tears of pain came to my eyes.

It might have been an hour before she turned off the water and opened the bathroom door. I walked over and looked inside, through a papery fog of steam. She was sitting on the toilet wrapped in a towel, with her hair turbaned into another, her long legs crossed precisely as she filed her fingernails.

"Had a good shower?"

"I'm getting married," she said, and she looked straight at me with a cool candor I remembered.

"Who is the man?"

"He's—older than me. He made his money in the computer business. Now he lives in the Oakland Hills, investing in software companies. I'm taking classes—studying to be a programmer. I met him at a conference in Santa Cruz."

"Are you happy?"

She shrugged. "I think I'll be all right with Caleb."

"Oh."

"Any motherly advice for me?"

When I did not reply immediately, we both felt uncomfortable. Ruth tilted her head in a brief, coquettish glance that I had never seen before. It was like her fluttering hand in the door; she seemed to have acquired a set of mannerisms, a new method of communication, and I had no idea what she wanted.

"No," I finally managed. "No advice."

I remembered my own mother, the way she had often known my desires and fears before I knew them myself. I had run away from her, but we had never really lost each other; even in this country, I had felt that she was holding me in her hands. I had never felt as estranged from her as my daughters had grown from me. Somehow I had lost both of my daughters. If I had learned English, I wondered, would I have been able to follow them? I will never know. But my daughters turned into women and I was left behind, stumbling after their voices.

I said, "Please stay for a few days. I want to know—"

"Mom, Caleb is waiting for me in France."

"Ruth—"

"I have my own life."

"Are you in love with him?"

"I don't know what you mean," she answered easily. "I don't know what you mean by love."

I blurted, "You were loved. You have been loved."

She took a deep, straining breath. I saw that it had taken courage for her to return, even to start this conversation, and I respected her for it. "I know," she said. "But I don't trust that kind of feeling." Her voice, so lovely and melodic, rough from smoking, cuts into my memory. "How could he have been that way with me? How could he have been so cruel?"

"There was more to him, more to his life," I whispered. "You just didn't see it."

She leaned forward and her tears fell onto her bare

toes. They were painted with a chipped, red polish, but they were the exact shape of her father's toes. Her voice was shaking when she spoke. "No, I didn't see it."

A FEW months later, Anna earned her master's degree in Asian Studies. I brought her here for a home-cooked meal. She looked exhausted, worn out from exams, raw-boned, with rough hair, her cuticles chewed ragged. She sat opposite me at the dinner table in her black rayon dress and stockings, and she said it might be better for her to do her Ph.D. at a school away from home, at Berkeley or Michigan. Then she ate a mouthful of rice. Controlled and easy, matter-of-fact, but the tips of her chopsticks trembled as they left her mouth, and when she saw my face, her lips twitched with a mutinous joy. It was true; I had taken her for granted.

After dinner, I went to her room. She sat reading in the bottom bunk; she had clipped a little lamp onto the bedpost.

"You're right," I said. "I think it would be a good experience for you."

She lifted her face to mine with sudden remorse, but her eyes immediately narrowed. Only between mothers and daughters, I think, can this change from anger to regret and back to anger mean so much and yet so little, in the scheme of things.

"You can't make me stay." I had never heard this from Anna.

"Who—who said I will make you stay?" I took a deep breath to control my voice. I had told her of Ruth's brief visit; she had accepted the news quietly, but afterwards, a kind of painful dignity had come into her solitary trips to see me, as if she felt, for some reason, that she had been passed over once again. "You deserve your time away. But promise one thing," I told her. "Promise you will come back home sometimes, on your vacations."

She kept her gaze on the bunk above, studying the shadows there. "I'll visit. I'm not like Ruth. I can't afford to play fast and loose with the only family I've got left. I'm not special enough for that."

Her voice seemed to throb and fill the room. "I felt glad when she left! At first I thought she should be forgiven for everything she did, because she was irresponsible, and irresponsible people can't be expected to do much, but after a while I understood that it wasn't irresponsibility—it was just selfishness. She was so selfish!

"When I was little I wanted her talent—I thought it would make Baba love me as much as he loved her. Then for a while I wanted her ability to turn away. As if she had no responsibility to anyone who loved her. I wished I could forget everything, forget the fights they used to have, forget about Baba."

"Is that what you still want?"

"No."

"What do you want?"

"Now, I just want—to know her. Just to be her friend."

We sat for what seemed an unremarkable length of time, given our lives together. When Anna spoke, her voice was shaking. "Don't cry, Mama, don't cry."

On the radio I have heard that the core of the earth is a ball of iron. It makes sense to me that there is such a fixed hardness at the center of things. In our family we seem destined to be drawn to this relentless core, but we so rarely speak about it. Now I regret that I did not try to talk to Anna about the fact that she and I had never chosen each other—this fact that lay always at the heart of things between us. Shortly after that conversation, the graduate school catalogues for Columbia and NYU appeared on the coffee table, on top of the others. There followed a few months of tranquil, quiet living with my daughter. I assumed there would be plenty of time ahead in which I could grow to understand her. I could foresee no more obstacles between Anna and me that would rival what had already come to pass.

But I had misunderstood again. What happened next came quietly, silently, overlooked despite my expectations. Beneath my shoulder blades in a place which is impossible to see and difficult to scratch, a small mole bloomed like an angry flower. I did not discover it until much time, too much time, had passed.

They say that nothing will illuminate a person like his body. The muscles of the back and neck reveal what he has hidden from himself. On Taiwan, I knew a Fujianese woman who was suddenly unable to digest asparagus. It had been her favorite food, but suddenly it was bringing on deep cramps that made her burst into tears. The doctors ran tests for ulcers, appendicitis, cancer. They found nothing; then one day she confided to a nurse that she had recently lost an unborn child. Afterwards she had no more stomach trouble, but she also lost her craving for asparagus and swore never to eat it again.

If what my mother says is true, all the unspoken thoughts of thirty years had been turned loose inside my body. They had taken on a prolific, tainted, microscopic life. At the time I couldn't swallow the truth of this; I still refuse. If this was true, then would my body's new growths not also have possessed a certain beauty? I think I should have also grown a pair of glistening, transparent and beautiful wings, like the wings of a sapphire dragonfly, exactly in the spot where the melanoma surfaced. There would have been the outward form of all the love and hope and real goodwill I gave to my husband and my children.

Also, my oncologist said that my mother's theory wasn't true.

The Saturday morning after the diagnosis of cancer had been made, Anna sat down across from me at the kitchen table. I was counting out my pills. Suddenly I had to take a dozen pills a day, some deadly and some strengthening. Some of them counteracted the side effects caused by the others. It calmed me to divide them into seven paper cups, to focus on their different colors and sizes, from a bullet-sized purple medication to a clear, soft golden vitamin pill that I found almost enchanting.

Anna said she had changed her mind, had decided to stay on and earn her doctorate with her department at Columbia.

"You go ahead, Anna. I'll be fine." I wanted her to stay with me, but I also wanted her to leave. Her leaving would be proof, I thought, that things were just the same, that we could get along in the same old way. And I was suddenly too tired or scared to fight—I didn't want to give her another reason to be angry at me.

But Anna put her palms on the table and examined her hands and she said, "No, I have to stay."

"I'll be all right," I said.

"Don't leave me, Mama. Don't leave me too!"

I had not expected this from her, although I have thought of it so often ever since that it has become like the core of me.

"I won't," I told her. And I did not plan to. I was still a youthful woman, forty-nine. I had seen too much of leaving. I had deserted Ruth, but I would not desert her sister. I never wanted to leave Anna, although even now she still believes I loved Ruth best. I did not want to leave even after I grew tired of counting out the pills; not even after we learned about the unfortunate outcome of the surgery, or after the bedroom air grew stifling with the foul smell of tumors.

When the moment came, I kept my eyes wide open, focused on my daughter's face. She bent over me, her shoulders hunched with grief and pity; then her small eyes widened in shock and fear, and I knew that I was dying. Until I saw her fear, I had not believed that I would die. It was true; it would happen. There came into my whole body a sudden feeling of surprise, like a flavor in my mouth. I felt the world spinning, as if I were being inexorably spun away from it. My body was being left behind. The room dimmed, the sounds of traffic ceased. The world's winds took hold of me. The earth began to rush below, and I who had once dreamed of leaving Brooklyn—I decided I would not let go. I held on like a metal filing, bracing myself against the force of the earth. I held on. I will not leave. I have held on, to this day.

FOR years, Anna planned to flee the house. I know this, for I spied her glossy decorating magazines, although she hid them under schoolbooks, tried to keep them away from me. The magazines were filled with photographs of empty rooms: kitchens, bedrooms, breakfast nooks, each wall covered with framed paintings, each table holding a vase of flowers. Strangers' houses, comforting because they held no past, meant to be viewed exactly in the moment. Living in these photographs, my daughter would finish her night of studying and walk to an imaginary bedroom, perhaps a vast loft, perhaps a small, high-ceilinged chamber of a Manhattan townhouse, with its narrow, antique wrought-iron bed and deep comforter of down.

She wanted to start fresh, release her punishing ties

to our old place, its floorboards warped from decades of unhappiness. On Saturday mornings she sat in Tian's old armchair, scanning ads. She hired a real estate agent, a thin, impeccably dressed man close to her in age, prematurely balding, with a tenor voice that rose in strained enthusiasm, only to deflate with sighs as time went by and she refused to take one apartment, then another. An old high school, converted to condominiums, soothed her with its smooth oak floors, but she finally said no—she thought the ceilings were too high; she found them threatening in their vastness of intention.

One day she opened the door to a brisk young couple full of plans, the woman's belly swollen with hope like freshly risen dough. They wandered our rooms with impersonal interest, looking past the faded prints and furniture, their x-ray happiness beaming through the walls as if they could see the place blown barren, faded clean and ready for change. Anna watched them with an expression of barely quelled surprise—could they not see the dingy cobwebs of our long-endured unhappiness? They bid, and Anna refused to sell. The agent's sighs grew yet more vast and airy until he disappeared.

Through these negotiations, I stayed silent. I had no desire to bend her thoughts; I had seen what that could do. But I might not have been careful enough. I think Anna could hear me, feel my desire that she stay. She is not certain I am watching her, although she has suspicions. I try to conceal myself, but my desires seep through the rooms, they flavor the air, they move like molecules in her blood.

On the day she earned her Ph.D., she came home from the ceremony, removed her heavy robe, and, wearing her graduation dress, climbed up on a chair and pulled down all our faded curtains. She piled them into plastic lawn bags, along with the cushions from the living room couch. Still wearing her stockings and high-heeled shoes, she dragged the bags down the stairs and hoisted them into the dumpster.

She hauled an old brass urn onto the fire escape and set to work burning the boxes of cancelled checks that we had stacked in our dresser drawers. The accounts had long been closed. There were boxes and boxes, dating from the late sixties, when Tian and I had just been married, and there was a check made out to a Brooklyn hospital the month after Anna's birth for thirty-five dollars and sixty-nine cents. The Immigration and Naturalization Service, seventeen dollars. Sears, Roebuck and Company, for the purchase of baby clothes, two dollars. The flames took slowly at first, then greedily, sending smoke into the night. She tipped the ashes between the iron slats of the fire escape and let them fall.

Workmen came in the next few weeks and dragged away the sagging, battered furniture. They ripped out the kitchen stove and sink, replacing them with sleek new appliances, white counter tops, glass surfaces. Anna put in a smooth, pale maple floor that ran through every room in the house. Finally, she had the workers lay in bathroom tiles the pale green of ancient celadon jars.

She repainted the long, narrow bedroom I had shared with Tian. The walls became blue, the ceiling white. She ordered a great bed that filled up one whole side, a simple bed with a walnut frame, and piled it with white comforters. On a small table she set a china lamp, a scarlet jewelbox.

Now Anna works at a nonprofit organization called the Asia Culture Institute, and she collects old Chinese furniture, elegantly shaped rosewood pieces to complement the spareness of her pale, plain walls. Her coffee table, which she never puts her feet upon, is a low K'ang table with graceful legs that curve out, then in, ending in what are called "horse's hooves." Her desk is a late-Qing rosewood version of a western desk. Her dishes are a simple rice pattern, the kind in which the rice-shaped designs become translucent when the bowls are lifted to the light.

Anna walks through the apartment in stocking feet, round-limbed, a little softer than she used to be, a little further into womanhood. She makes for herself the sort of thoughtful, savory dishes I have always made, although she uses odd vegetables in her stirfries and she has learned to cook with Indian spices. She writes occasionally, in Chinese, to her great-aunt, my mother's sister, still living in Taiwan. And always there is that watchfulness in her manner that Tian and I observed when she was only a tiny child.

Unlike Ruth, she seems to have no need for any company other than friendship. A round-faced friend from graduate school has on occasion come over in the evening to watch videotapes of Chinese movies. Anna enjoys his company, and sometimes he does not leave until early morning. But in those moments when some change in the mood between them might take place, when they have discussed a film they've just enjoyed, after laughter or an unexpected confession brings an expectant silence to the room, he will look at her with some confusion. Anna will at such moments refuse to meet his eye; she will scowl briefly at her hands and plunge back into the conversation. Watching her I wonder this: How long must we wait to outlast sorrow?

MANY years ago, after we made love, Tian told me the story of his escape from the mainland, to Taiwan. We lay in his tiny music room, safe inside the heart of this house, and the city sounds floated far away and the traffic seemed like music to me. I remember I had nothing on my mind—for once, no fears. I was simply breathing in the air, with his smell in it, and the scent of the cleaning fluid we had gotten on our hands that day as we fixed up the room. The long evening light filtered through the living room curtains, making a patch of rippled gold on the hallway floor.

"I left China in the middle of the night," Tian said. He explained he'd had a plan to swim half a mile across the Taiwan Strait to a refugee ship. He swam on his side and held his violin above the water, his head tilted so he could watch for the ship, the *Sonya*, which waited off the Fujian coast, a dark shape against the stars.

Before setting off, he removed the violin's strings, pegs, bridge, soundpost, and tailpiece, and placed them with the rosin in a packet of canvas and oilcloth. He tied this packet, and his horsehair bow, to the instrument and wrapped everything again in canvas and oilcloth. He expected to make the trip on his right side and switch only if necessary. He was not a powerful man, but tensile and fluidly muscled. Moreover, he had trained himself over many years of playing his instrument to hold his left arm in the air. Aside from the violin, bow, and rosin, he carried only his fee for passage to Taiwan and the clothes on his back.

I still imagine him moving quietly and deliberately over the water, buoyed under the moonless sky. He had chosen to flee on the night of a new moon because he knew the coast was fairly lit with eyes, those of civilians as well as of Communist patrols. The warm waves broke gently over his body like black, wet sleep. He struggled slowly toward the silhouette of the refugee ship, the *Sonya*, his throat dried hollow with seawater, his left arm numb from holding up the instrument. At one point, he slowed and floated in the waves, fitted the familiar shape against his chin, as if he were considering a melody. But he only rested for a moment.

The ship loomed closer. The *Sonya* had been purchased from Russia by the Chinese government at the turn of the century. It had changed hands several times during the tumultuous warlord era and was finally sold to a merchant with ties to the underworld. It waited, low in the water, heavy with human cargo. Tian summoned his deepest voice and shouted, "*Wei!*"

The reply came back, "We have no more room!"

Tian shouted, "I have double the cash!" and after a few long minutes, treading water, he made out the splash of a rope ladder and struggled toward it. He slung the violin over his back and climbed the ladder, willing his trembling left arm to strength. Above, he could see the shadows of arms and hands, reaching for his payment—passage for a man and one small bundle. They refused to let him on board until they had counted the money.

No one asked what was in his oddly-shaped sack. I suppose they had seen so many people passing through that even the most unusual items—live animals, bags of bones—were no longer remarkable. One woman aboard his ship had only a potted orange tree. Exhausted, dripping, he wedged himself into a space on the crowded deck and set to work unwrapping the instrument. He smelled and heard human fear and grief pressed all around him, but he ignored everything, holding onto his own tight, shining wire of hope and plans. He took out the violin and carefully touched and tasted the chin rest, the scroll, the tip of the bow, for any hint of salt or moisture. He had long, square-tipped fingers, a musician's fingers, and they trembled as they traced the curves of the belly. He rewrapped the instrument and bow in canvas, set the bundle carefully between his knees, then spread the oilcloth over all, pulling it up around his chin. Then he leaned his head against the silent bulk of another passenger, and closed his eyes. Wind stirred the heavy wet hair that fell across his forehead. Deep below he felt a shudder as the ship began to move. Triumphantly, he slept.

I remember the lonely sound of Tian's voice as he told me about this journey, the light dimming in the small room, the sounds of traffic from the avenue. How I had yearned for him then! I had been certain there would be more stories, that soon enough I would know everything about his life. I did not know that this would be the end of the stories, and that everything afterward would have to be searched out, scratched out in deep wounds.

I did not know when I put Tian's hat in his hands that I would spend my life with a man I could never make happy. If I had known what I know now, would I have gone ahead and married him? I ponder the stories of my daughters. It seems to me that love is best entered unaware; it best happens without thought, like a sudden plunge into deep water.

I think of Ruth, scoured clean by her hot shower and wrapped in towels, saying, "I don't trust that kind of feeling." I watch Anna move through her careful, quiet life, resolutely turning away from what is offered to her. Is it that she doesn't recognize the possibility of love? Does she expect it to arrive in some different shape, or sound, or coloring? Perhaps Ruth and Anna are more alike than they realize. Their choices are attempts to escape an attachment overpowering enough to destroy them unless they refuse it.

In Beijing, a boy takes music lessons from a German tutor who presents him with the gift of a violin. A slender-bellied instrument, with a rich, brown color and golden ribs that shimmer on its back. Later, a young man swims into the sea, holding a precious bundle in one hand above the darkened water. He gasps; he struggles onto a ship. As I imagine this, I feel a powerful urge to hide him: from those whom he has left behind forever; from the anxious souls surrounding him; from the few people in Taipei whose names and addresses he has memorized, people unaware of his imminent arrival. I want him to get away, escape his life, even though I know that he will not escape, cannot escape the punishment that invariably comes to people who dare to dream such flagrant and extravagant designs. I cannot hide him. Even the ancient broken ship, the *Sonya,* with her vast indifference—how could she, I think, have failed to creak and shudder beneath the weight of this man's desire? The immensity of such hunger, folded into his cloth shelter, waiting in the middle of the sea.

THERE are things that cannot be changed. The sound of rain as it strikes a roof cannot be altered as long as the roof remains. Anna cannot bend the angle of sunlight through the kitchen window. I saw the workmen struggle to remove my daughters' bunk bed. It took an hour to pound the metal joints out of their battered fittings. They used hammers. They had to bend the frame and ruin the bed in order to take it apart. Now the room is empty; the newly painted lilac walls are bare except for a painting of two fir trees under snow. The bedroom window, like all the windows in the place, is old and has no screen. In the winter they waste energy, and Anna has looked into having them replaced, but the other owners of the building are avoiding the job, since it is troublesome and expensive. The neighborhood has been declared a historic district, and all structural changes are subject to guidelines.

So it is still possible for an agile person to open the bedroom window, step out to the fire escape, and climb up on the roof to sit and look across the river at the gray or glittering cutout of Manhattan. A person could still jiggle the kitchen window in a certain way and reenter from the platform. I am waiting; every day I wait in hope that this will come to pass. More than anything, I want my daughters to meet again.

I wait, I listen in the night. Music lingers in these walls, uncoiling in the space between the kitchen and the practice room, moving through the hall in wisps and strands of melody. I hear the high, throbbing sounds rising up through the heating vents like a woman's voice. Blunt chords of anger, fragile notes that barely whisper. I hear the sorrow that seems to run in all our blood, and also an unbreakable thread of love. Through all this, Anna sleeps; but on some nights, as the melodies fade away, she shudders and sits up in bed. The faint light reveals her look of bleak confusion. Perhaps she has been dreaming of her greatest hope and fear—that the house is gone, that it is destroyed, and nothing more remains of it. This is an echo of my own fear: that there might come a time when no one on earth will remember our lives.

Hunger

WATER NAMES

SUMMERTIME AT DUSK WE'D GATHER on the back porch, tired and sticky from another day of fierce encoded quarrels, nursing our mosquito bites and frail dignities, sisters in name only. At first we'd pinch and slap each other, fighting for the best—least ragged—folding chair. Then we'd argue over who would sit next to our grandmother. We were so close together on the tiny porch that we often pulled our own hair by mistake. Forbidden to bite, we planted silent toothmarks on each others' wrists. We ignored the bulk of house behind us, the yard, the fields, the darkening sky. We even forgot about our grandmother. Then suddenly we'd hear her old, dry voice, very close, almost on the backs of our necks.

"*Xiushila*! Shame on you. Fighting like a bunch of chickens."

And Ingrid, the oldest, would freeze with her thumb and forefinger right on the back of Lily's arm. I would slide my hand away from the end of Ingrid's braid. Ashamed, we would shuffle our feet while Waipuo calmly found her chair.

On some nights she sat with us in silence, the tip of her cigarette glowing red like a distant stoplight. But on some nights she told us stories, "just to keep up your Chinese," she said, and the red dot flickered and danced, making ghostly shapes as she moved her hands like a magician in the dark.

"In these prairie crickets I often hear the sound of rippling waters, of the Yangtze River," she said. "Granddaughters, you are descended on both sides from people of the water country, near the mouth of the great Chang Jiang, as it is called, where the river is so grand and broad that even on clear days you can scarcely see the other side.

"The Chang Jiang runs four thousand miles, originating in the Himalaya mountains where it crashes, flecked with gold dust, down steep cliffs so perilous and remote that few humans have ever seen them. In central China, the river squeezes through deep gorges, then widens in its last thousand miles to the sea. Our ancestors have lived near the mouth of this river, the ever-changing delta, near a city called Nanjing, for more than a thousand years."

"A thousand years," murmured Lily, who was only ten. When she was younger she had sometimes burst into nervous crying at the thought of so many years. Her small insistent fingers grabbed my fingers in the dark.

"Through your mother and I you are descended from a line of great men and women. We have survived countless floods and seasons of ill-fortune because we have the spirit of the river in us. Unlike mountains, we cannot be powdered down or broken apart. Instead, we run together, like raindrops. Our strength and spirit wear down mountains into sand. But even our people must respect the water."

She paused, and a bit of ash glowed briefly as it drifted to the floor.

"When I was young, my own grandmother once told me the story of Wen Zhiqing's daughter. Twelve hundred years ago the civilized parts of China still lay to the north, and the Yangtze valley lay unspoiled. In those days lived an ancestor named Wen Zhiqing, a resourceful man, and proud. He had been fishing for many years with trained cormorants, which you girls of course have never seen. Cormorants are sleek, black birds with long, bending necks which the fishermen fitted with metal rings so the fish they caught could not be swallowed. The birds would perch on the side of the old wooden boat and dive into the river." We had only known blue swimming pools, but we tried to imagine the sudden shock of cold and the plunge, deep into water.

"Now, Wen Zhiqing had a favorite daughter who was very beautiful and loved the river. She would beg to go out on the boat with him. This daughter was a restless one, never contented with their catch, and often she insisted they stay out until it was almost dark. Even then, she was not satisfied. She had been spoiled by her father, kept protected from the river, so she could not see its danger. To this young woman, the river was as familiar as the sky. It was a bright, broad road stretching out to curious lands. She did not fully understand the river's depths.

"One clear spring evening, as she watched the last bird dive off into the blackening waters, she said, 'If only this catch would bring back something more than another fish!'

"She leaned over the side of the boat and looked at the water. The stars and moon reflected back at her. And it is said that the spirits living underneath the water looked up at her as well. And the spirit of a young man who had drowned in the river many years before saw her lovely face."

We had heard about the ghosts of the drowned,

who wait forever in the water for a living person to pull down instead. A faint breeze moved through the mosquito screens and we shivered.

"The cormorant was gone for a very long time," Waipuo said, "so long that the fisherman grew puzzled. Then, suddenly, the bird emerged from the waters, almost invisible in the night. Wen Zhiqing grasped his catch, a very large fish, and guided the boat back to shore. And when Wen reached home, he gutted the fish and discovered, in its stomach, a valuable pearl ring."

"From the man?" said Lily.

"Sshh, she'll tell you."

Waipuo ignored us. "His daughter was delighted that her wish had been fulfilled. What most excited her was the idea of an entire world like this, a world where such a beautiful ring would be only a bauble! For part of her had always longed to see faraway things and places. The river had put a spell on her heart. In the evenings she began to sit on the bank, looking at her own reflection in the water. Sometimes she said she saw a handsome young man looking back at her. And her yearning for him filled her heart with sorrow and fear, for she knew that she would soon leave her beloved family.

"'It's just the moon,' said Wen Zhiqing, but his daughter shook her head. 'There's a kingdom under the water,' she said. 'The prince is asking me to marry him. He sent the ring as an offering to you.' 'Nonsense,' said her father, and he forbade her to sit by the water again.

"For a year things went as usual, but the next spring there came a terrible flood that swept away almost everything. In the middle of a torrential rain, the family noticed that the daughter was missing. She had taken advantage of the confusion to hurry to the river and visit her beloved. The family searched for days but they never found her."

Hunger

Her smoky, rattling voice came to a stop.

"What happened to her?" Lily said.

"It's okay, stupid," I told her. "She was so beautiful that she went to join the kingdom of her beloved. Right?"

"Who knows?" Waipuo said. "They say she was seduced by a water ghost. Or perhaps she lost her mind to desiring."

"What do you mean?" asked Ingrid.

"I'm going inside," Waipuo said, and got out of her chair with a creak. A moment later the light went on in her bedroom window. We knew she stood before the mirror, combing out her long, wavy silver-gray hair, and we imagined that in her youth she too had been beautiful.

We sat together without talking, breathing our dreams in the lingering smoke. We had gotten used to Waipuo's abruptness, her habit of creating a question and leaving without answering it, as if she were disappointed in the question itself. We tried to imagine Wen Zhiqing's daughter. What did she look like? How old was she? Why hadn't anyone remembered her name?

While we weren't watching, the stars had emerged. Their brilliant pinpoints mapped the heavens. They glittered over us, over Waipuo in her room, the house, and the small city we lived in, the great waves of grass that ran for miles around us, the ground beneath as dry and hard as bone.

SAN

MY FATHER LEFT MY MOTHER AND ME one rainy summer morning, carrying a new umbrella of mine. From our third-floor window I watched him close the front door and pause to glance at the sky. Then he opened my umbrella. I liked the big red flower pattern—it was *fuqi*, prosperous—but in the hands of a man, even a handsome man like my father, the umbrella looked gaudy and ridiculous. Still, he did not hunch underneath but carried it high up, almost jauntily.

As I watched him walk away, I remembered a Chinese superstition. The Mandarin word for umbrella, *san*, also means "to fall apart." If you acquire an umbrella without paying for it, your life will fall apart. My father had scoffed at such beliefs. The umbrella had been a present from him. Now I stood and watched it go, bright and ill-fated like so many of his promises.

Later that morning the roof of our apartment sprang a leak. Two tiles buckled off the kitchen floor, revealing a surprising layer of mud, as if my mother's mopping over the years had merely pushed the dirt beneath the tiles and all along we'd been living over a floor of soot.

My mother knelt with a sponge in one hand. She wouldn't look at me. Her heavy chignon had come undone and a thick lock of hair wavered down her back.

"Can I help?" I asked, standing over her. She did not answer but stroked the tiles with her sponge.

I put the big rice cooker underneath the leak. Then I went to my room. All morning, I studied problems for my summer school math class. I heard my mother, in the kitchen, start to sob. I felt only fear—a dense stone in my chest—but I put even this aside so I could study. My father had taught me to focus on the equations in front of me, and so I spent the hours after he left thinking about trigonometry, a subject he had loved.

MY mathematical talent had sprung from an early backwardness. As a child I could not count past three: my father, my mother, and me.

"Caroline is making progress in her English lessons, but she remains baffled by the natural numbers," read an early report card. "She cannot grasp the *countability* of blocks and other solid objects. For this reason I am recommending that she repeat the first grade."

This comment left my father speechless. He believed I was a brilliant child. And mathematics had been his favorite subject back in China, before political trouble had forced him to quit school and, eventually, the country.

"*Counting*," he said in English, when he was able to talk again. His dark eyebrows swooped over the bridge of his acquiline nose. Despite his drastic ups and downs, bad news always caught him by surprise. But he recovered with typical buoyancy. "Don't worry, Lily," he told my mother.

"It's those western teachers. *I'll* teach her how to count."

And so my father, himself an unreliable man, taught me to keep track of things. We counted apples, bean sprouts, grains of rice. I learned to count in pairs, with ivory chopsticks. We stood on the corner of Atlantic Avenue, counting cars to learn big numbers. We spent a lovely afternoon in Prospect Park, counting blades of grass aloud until we both had scratchy throats.

"Keep going," he urged me on as the shadows lengthened. "I want you to be able to count all the money I'm going to make, here in America."

By the time I was seven I had learned the multiplication tables to twenty-times-twenty. In the following year I learned to recite the table of squares and the table of cubes, both so quickly that the words blended together into a single stream, almost meaningless: "Oneeighttwentysevensixtyfouronetwentyfivetwosixteenthreefortythree . . ."

As I chanted, my father would iron the white shirt and black trousers he wore to his waiter's job, a "temporary" job. Or he stood in the kitchen, Mondays off, with three blue balls and one red ball, juggling expertly beneath the low tin ceiling. Each time the red ball reached his hand I was ordered to stress a syllable. Thus "One, *eight*, twenty-*sev*en, sixty-*four*."

"Pro*nounce*," said my father, proud of his clear r's. To succeed in America, he was sure, required good pronunciation as well as math. He often teased my mother for pronouncing my name *Calorin*, "like a diet formula," he said. They had named me Caroline after Caroline Kennedy, who was born shortly before their arrival in the States. After all, my father's name was Jack. And if the name was good enough for a president's daughter, then certainly it was good enough for me.

HUNGER

AFTER I learned to count I began, belatedly, to notice things. Signs of hard luck and good fortune moved through our apartment like sudden storms. A pale stripe on my father's tanned wrist revealed where his watch had been. A new pair of aquamarine slippers shimmered on my mother's feet. A beautiful collection of fourteen cacti, each distinct, bloomed on our fire escape for several summer months and then vanished.

I made careful explorations of our apartment. At the back of the foyer closet, inside the faded red suitcase my mother had brought from China, I discovered a cache of little silk purses wrapped in a cotton shirt. When I heard her footsteps I instinctively closed the suitcase and pretended I was looking for a pair of mittens. Then I went to my room and shut the door, slightly dizzy with anticipation and guilt.

A few days later when my mother was out, I opened one purse. Inside was a swirling gold pin with pearl and coral flowers. I made many secret visits to the closet, a series of small sins. Each time I opened one more treasure. There were bright green, milky white, and carmine bracelets. Some of the bracelets were so small I could not fit them over my hand. There was a ring with a pearl as big as a marble. A strand of pearls, each the size of a large pea. A strand of jade beads carved in the shape of small buddhas. A rusty key.

"Do you still have keys to our old house in China?" I asked my father.

"That's the past, Caroline," he said. "*Wanle.* It is gone."

Surrounded by questions, I became intrigued by the answers to things. My report cards showed that I became a good student, a very good student, particularly in math. At twelve, I was the only person from my class to test into a public school for the gifted in Manhattan. My father attended the school event where this news was announced. I remember his pleased expression as we approached the small, crowded auditorium. He had piled all of our overcoats and his fedora over one arm, but with the other he opened the door for my mother and me. As I filed past he raised his eyebrows and nodded — proud, but not at all surprised by my achievement.

HE believed in the effortless, in splurging and quick riches. While I studied, bent and dogged, and my mother hoarded things, my father strayed from waitering and turned to something bigger. He had a taste for making deals, he said to us. A nose for good investments. Some friends were helping him. He began to stay out late and come home with surprises. On good nights, he brought us presents: a sewing kit, a pink silk scarf. Once he climbed out of a taxicab with a hundred silver dollars in my old marble bag.

On bad nights, my father whistled his way home. I sometimes woke to his high music floating from the street. I sat up and spied at him through the venetian blind. He no longer wore his waiter's clothes; his overcoat was dark. I could just make out the glitter of his shiny shoes. He stepped lightly, always, on bad nights, although he'd whistled clear across the bridge to save on subway fare. He favored Stephen Foster tunes and Broadway musicals. He flung his head back on a long, pure note. When he reached our door he stood still for a moment and squared his shoulders.

My mother, too, knew what the whistling meant.

"Stayed up for me?"

"I wasn't tired."

I crept to my door to peek at them. My mother staring at her feet. My father's hopeful face, his exaggerated brightness. My mother said, "Go to sleep, Caroline."

But I had trouble sleeping. I could feel him slipping

away from us, drifting far in search of some intoxicating music. Each time he wandered off, it seemed to take more effort to recall us. He began to speak with his head cocked, as if listening for something. He often stood at the living room window, staring at the street.

"Does Baba have a new job?" I asked my mother.

"No." She looked away.

I felt sorry I'd asked. Questions caused my mother pain. But I was afraid to ask my father. In his guarded face he held a flaming knowledge: a kind of faith, a glimpse of opportunities that lay beyond my understanding.

ALL that year I hunted clues, made lists of evidence.

Missing on February 3:
> *carved endtable*
> *painting of fruit (from front hallway)*
> *jade buddha*
> *camera (mine)*

I followed him. One evening after I missed my camera, I heard the front door slam. I grabbed my coat and bolted down the stairs. I dodged across the street half a block back, peering around pedestrians and traffic signs, my eyes fixed on his overcoat and fedora. At the subway station I waited by the token booth and dashed into the bright car behind him, keeping track of his shiny shoes through the swaying windows. I almost missed him when he left the train. Outside it was already dusk. The tall, cold shapes of City Hall and the courthouses loomed over us and I followed at a distance. I felt light as a puff of silk, breathing hard, excited, almost running.

Past the pawn shops, the off-track betting office with its shuffling line of men in old overcoats, toward the dirty, crowded streets of Chinatown, its neon signs winking on for the night. Groups of teenagers, chattering in Cantonese, looked strangely at me and kept walking.

"Incense, candles, incense, *xiaojie*?" A street vendor held a grimy handful toward me.

"No, thanks," I panted. I almost lost him but then ahead I recognized his elegant stride. He turned into a small, shabby building, nodding to an old man who stood at the door. I hung around outside, stamping my shoes on the icy sidewalk.

After a minute the old man walked over to me. "Your father does not know you followed him," he told me in Chinese. "You must go home. Go home, and I will not tell him you were here."

For a minute I couldn't move. He was exactly my height. His short hair was white but his forehead strangely unlined, his clothes well-made. It was his expensive tweed overcoat that made me turn around. That and the decaying, fetid odor of his teeth, and the fact that he knew my father well enough to recognize my features, knew he would not have wanted me to follow him. I reboarded the train at the Canal Street station. Back in the apartment, I stayed up until well past midnight, but I didn't hear him come home.

I DIDN'T need to follow him. I should have known that eventually he would show his secret to me, his one pupil. A few months later, on the night before my fourteenth birthday, he motioned me to stay seated after supper. The hanging lamp cast a circle of light over the worn kitchen table.

"I'm going to teach you some math," he said.

I glanced at his face, but his eyes glowed black and expressionless in their sockets, hollow in the lamplight.

Over his shoulder I saw my mother check to see that we were occupied. Then she walked into the foyer and opened the closet door, where the jewelry was. I felt a tingle of fear, even though I had concealed my visits perfectly.

"Concentrate," said my father. "Here is a penny. Each penny has two sides: heads and tails. You understand me, Caroline?"

I nodded. The dull coin looked like a hole in his palm.

"*Hao*," he said: good. His brown hand danced and the penny flipped onto the table. Heads. "Now, if I throw this coin many many times, how often would I get heads?"

"One-half of the time."

He nodded.

"*Hao*," he said. "That is the *huo ran lu*. The *huo ran lu* for heads is one-half. If you know that, you can figure out the *huo ran lu* that I will get two heads if I throw twice in a row." He waited a minute. "Think of it as a limiting of possibilities. The first throw cuts the possibilities in half."

I looked into the dark tunnel of my father's eyes and, following the discipline of his endless drilling, I began to understand where we had been going. Counting, multiplication, the table of squares. "Half of the half," I said. "A quarter."

He set the coins aside and reached into his shirt pocket. Suddenly, with a gesture of his hand, two dice lay in the middle of the yellow circle of light. Two small chunks of ivory, with tiny black pits in them.

"Count the sides," he said.

The little cube felt cold and heavy. "Six."

My father's hand closed over the second die. "What is the *huo ran lu* that I will get a side with only two dots?"

My mind wavered in surprise at his intensity. But I knew the answer. "One-sixth," I said.

He nodded. "You are a smart daughter," he said.

I discovered that I had been holding onto the table leg with my left hand, and I let go. I heard the creak of the hall closet door but my father did not look away from the die in his hand.

"What is the *huo ran lu* that I can roll the side with two dots twice in a row?" he said.

"One thirty-sixth."

"Three times in a row?"

"One two-hundred-and-sixteenth."

"That is very good!" he said. "Now, the *huo ran lu* that I will be able to roll a two is one-sixth. Would it be a reasonable bet that I will not roll a two?"

I nodded.

"We could say, if I roll a two, you may have both pennies."

I saw it then, deep in his eyes—a spark of excitement, a piece of joy particularly his. It was there for an instant and disappeared. He frowned and nodded toward the table as if to say: pay attention. Then his hand flourished and the die trickled into the light. I bent eagerly over the table, but my father sat perfectly still, impassive. Two dots.

When I looked up at him in astonishment I noticed my mother, standing in the doorway, her two huge eyes burning in her white face.

"Jack."

My father started, but he didn't turn around to look at her. "Yes, Lily," he said.

The die grew wet in my hand.

"What are you doing?"

"Giving the child a lesson."

"And what is she going to learn from this?" My mother's voice trembled but it did not rise. "Where will she go with this?"

"Lily," my father said.

"What will become of us?" my mother almost whispered. She looked around the kitchen. Almost all of the furniture had disappeared. The old kitchen table and the three chairs, plus our rice cooker, were virtually the only things left in the room.

I grabbed the second die and left the table. In my room as I listened to my parents next door in the kitchen I rolled one die two hundred and sixteen times, keeping track by making marks on the back of a school notebook. But I failed to reach a two more than twice in a row.

"The suitcase, Jack. Where is it?"

After a moment my father muttered, "I'll get it back. Don't you believe me?"

"I don't know." She began to cry so loudly that even though I pressed my hands against my ears I could still hear her. My father said nothing. I hunched down over my knees, trying to shut them out.

"You promised me, you promised me you'd never touch them!"

"I was going to bring them back!"

"We have nothing for Caroline's birthday . . . "

Something crashed against the other side of my bedroom wall. I scuttled to the opposite wall and huddled in the corner of my bed.

For a long period after I heard nothing but my mother's sobbing. Then they left the kitchen. The house was utterly silent. I realized I had wrapped my arms around my knees to keep from trembling. I felt strange and light-headed: oh, but I understood now. My father was a gambler, a *dutu*, an apprentice of chance. Of course.

With the understanding came a desperate need to see both of them. I stood up and walked through the living room to my parents' bedroom. The door was ajar. I peered in.

The moonlight, blue and white, shifted and flickered on the bed, on my mother' s long black hair twisting over her arm. Her white fingers moved vaguely. I felt terrified for her. He moved against her body in such a consuming way, as if he might pass through her, as if she were incorporeal. I watched for several minutes before my mother made a sound that frightened me so much I had to leave.

THE next morning my eyes felt sandy and strange. We strolled down Atlantic Avenue, holding hands, with me in the middle because it was my birthday. My mother's stride was tentative, but my father walked with the calculated lightness and unconcern of one who has nothing in his pockets. Several gulls flew up before us, and he watched with delight as they wheeled into the cloudy sky. The charm of Brooklyn, this wide shabby street bustling with immigrants like ourselves, was enough to make him feel lucky.

He squeezed my hand, a signal that I should squeeze my mother's for him. We'd played this game many times over the years, but today I hesitated. My mother's hand did not feel like something to hold onto. Despite the warm weather her fingers in mine were cold. I squeezed, however, and she turned. He looked at her over the top of my head, and my mother, seeing his expression, lapsed into a smile that caused the Greek delivery boys from the corner pizza parlor to turn their heads as we passed. She and my father didn't notice.

We walked past a display of furniture on the sidewalk—incomplete sets of dining chairs, hat stands, old sewing tables—and I stared for a minute, for I thought I saw something standing behind a battered desk: a rosewood dresser my parents had brought from Taiwan; it used to be in my own bedroom. I once kept my dolls in the bottom left drawer, the one with the little scar where I had nicked it with a roller skate. . . . Perhaps it only had a similar shape. But it could very well be our dresser. I knew better than to point it out. I turned away.

Hunger

"Oh, Jack, the flowers!" my mother exclaimed in Chinese. She let go of my hand and rushed to DeLorenzio's floral display, sank down to smell the potted gardenias with a grace that brought my father and me to a sudden stop.

My father's black eyebrows came down over his eyes. "*Ni qu gen ni mama tan yi tan*, go talk to your mother," he said, giving me a little push. I frowned. "Go on."

She was speaking with Mr. DeLorenzio, and I stood instinctively on their far side, trying to act cute despite my age in order to distract them from what my father was doing. He stood before the red geraniums. He picked up a plant, considered it, and set it down with a critical shake of his head.

"And how are you today sweetheart?" Mr. DeLorenzio bent toward me, offering me a close-up of his gray handlebar moustache. Behind him, my father disappeared from view.

"She's shy," said my mother proudly. After a few minutes I tugged her sleeve, and she said goodbye to the florist. We turned, continued walking down the street.

"Where is your father?"

"I think he's somewhere up there."

I pulled her toward the corner. My father stepped out from behind a pet store, smiling broadly, holding the pot of geraniums.

"It's going to rain," he proclaimed, as if he'd planned it himself.

The drops felt light and warm on my face. We ran to the nearest awning, where my mother put on her rain bonnet. Then my father disappeared, leaving us standing on the sidewalk. I didn't notice him leave. All of a sudden he was just gone.

"Where's Baba?" I asked my mother.

"I don't know," she said, calmly tucking her hair into the plastic bonnet. The geraniums stood at her feet. I looked around us. The sidewalks had become slick and dark; people hurried along. The wind blew cool in my face. Then the revolving doors behind us whirled and my father walked out.

"There you are," my mother said.

"Here, Caroline," said my father to me. He reached into his jacket and pulled out the umbrella. It lay balanced on his palm, its brilliant colors neatly furled, an offering.

I wanted to refuse the umbrella. For a moment I believed that if I did, I could separate myself from both of my parents, and our pains, and everything that bound me to them.

I looked up at my father's face. He was watching me intently. I took the umbrella.

"Thanks," I said. He smiled. The next day, he was gone.

MY mother had her hair cut short and dressed in mourning colors; this attitude bestowed on her a haunting, muted beauty. She was hired for the lunch shift at a chic Manhattan Chinese restaurant. Our lives grew stable and very quiet. In the evenings I studied while my mother sat in the kitchen, waiting, cutting carrots and mushroom caps into elaborate shapes for our small stir-frys, or combining birdseed for the feeder on the fire escape in the exact proportions that my father had claimed would bring the most cardinals and the fewest sparrows. I did the homework for advanced placement courses. I planned to enter Columbia with the academic standing of a sophomore. We spoke gently to each other about harmless, tactful things. "Peanut sauce," we said. "Shopping." "Homework." "Apricots."

I studied trigonometry. I grew skillful in that subject without ever liking it. I learned calculus, linear algebra, and liked them less and less, but I kept studying, seeking the comfort that arithmetic had once provided. Things fall apart, it seems, with terrible slowness. I could not see that true mathematics, rather than keeping track of things, moves toward the unexplainable. A swooping line descends from nowhere, turns, escapes to some infinity. Centuries of scholars work to solve a single puzzle. In mathematics, as in love, the riddles matter most.

IN the months when I was failing out of Columbia, I spent a lot of my time on the subway. I rode to Coney Island, to the watery edge of Brooklyn, and stayed on the express train as it changed directions and went back deep under the river, into Manhattan. Around City Hall or 14th Street a few Chinese people always got on the train, and I sometimes saw a particular kind of man, no longer young but his face curiously unlined, wearing an expensive but shabby overcoat and shiny shoes. I would watch until he got off at his stop. Then I would sit back and wait as the train pulsed through the dark tunnels under the long island of Manhattan, and sometimes the light would blink out for a minute and I would see blue sparks shooting off the tracks. I was waiting for the moment around 125th Street where the express train rushed up into daylight. This sudden openness, this coming out of darkness into a new world, helped me understand how he must have felt. I imagined him bent over a pair of dice that glowed like tiny skulls under the yellow kitchen light. I saw him walking out the door with my flowery umbrella, pausing to look up at the sky and the innumerable, luminous possibilities that lay ahead.

THE
UNFORGETTING

ON THE SUMMER DAY IN 1967 WHEN
Ming Hwang first saw the eastern Iowa hills, he pulled
his car off the road and stopped the engine. He felt over-
whelmed, as if he had arrived once more at the sea that
he had crossed to reach America and his destiny lay again
upon some faraway shore. The neat, green fields rolled
out to meet the sky. The narrow strip of highway looked
barely navigable. Surely no Chinese man could ever have
laid eyes upon this place before.

Beside him, Sansan stirred and squinted into the hazy
light. "This is beautiful," she said. "Why did you stop?"

For a minute Ming could not reply. He wanted to say,
"This place has nothing to do with us." Instead, he pointed
out the windshield. "Do you see that water over there? That's
Mercy Lake. The town is only a mile away." He added,
"Maybe it will bring us luck."

When she didn't answer, he turned to examine her
smooth, brown face and knew that she also was afraid. He

Hunger

looked over his shoulder to make sure that Charles was still asleep and would not hear the conversation. "Is something wrong?" he asked.

"We're getting old," she said. "How will we make the space in our minds for everything we'll need to learn here?"

Without a pause, he answered her, "We will forget."

Sansan's dark eyes flickered; then she nodded. Ming glanced back again at his son. He turned the key in the ignition and fixed his gaze upon the road.

AND so the Hwangs forgot what they no longer needed. In the basement, inside the yellow carpetbag that Sansan had carried from Beijing, were six rice bowls that Sansan's mother said had once been used in the emperor's household. They were plain white bowls; Sansan said she thought they were only from the servants' quarters. Still, she had held onto them, imagining that their thin-edged beauty might sustain her when she grew tired of living in the present. But once the Hwangs had settled in Mercy Lake, she never used the bowls; she rarely even mentioned them.

They forgot what they could no longer bear to hope for. In the basement of their house, behind a sliding panel in his desk, stood Ming's old copy of the *Handbook of Chemistry and Physics*. It was the Twenty-sixth Edition, published in 1943, the only book that he had carried in his suitcase out of China. The *Handbook*'s deep brown cover was cracked and stained; its information had grown outdated. Ming had once believed that some day Charles might find it interesting, and so he had saved the heavy volume, even though its Periodic Table listed only ninety-two elements. In 1958, when Charles was born, the table of known elements had grown to 101, and Ming had lost track of chemistry, had given up his hope of studying science. In Mercy Lake he started his new job as a photocopy machine repairman, and the *Handbook* stayed on its shelf.

They learned what they needed to know. Photocopy machines were still so new that people had trouble maintaining them—mostly due to fear. They would call about the slightest problems: a toner cartridge, a paper jam. Ming possessed a delicate touch. He quickly grasped the ins and outs of the different models. He could sense which button or lever to press and how to get at the most difficult jams. While he fiddled around, a clerk or secretary often stood nearby, curious and wary, watching his face and hands, remarking on the infallibility and effectiveness of carbon paper. Ming would listen and nod, affecting sympathy, but privately he disagreed. He needed to believe in the future, when every office would have a new machine. And he found comfort in the presence of such effortless reproduction. He brought home photocopied samples to show Sansan how the machines could trace the shapes of drawings or letters, handwritten or typed. Sometimes, on the weekend, he took Charles to the office. To the inside cover of his logbook he taped a photocopy of Charles's little hand.

WHEN Charles finished fourth grade, the Hwangs received a letter from his teacher, Mrs. Carlsen. She said he was doing excellent work in math and science, but his vocabulary was below average. He also had trouble pronouncing words. Did they speak Chinese in their house? She suggested that they not require him to speak Chinese, for the time being at least.

"I *do* speak English," Ming insisted, after he and Sansan had told Charles his usual bedtime story and sent him off to bed.

Charles had always been quiet and slow to speak. But

Ming had assumed that he was cautious, reasoning out what he said. Now Ming began to worry that he might get lost between his two languages. The day after they received the letter, Ming came home early and watched Charles trudge up the driveway, his blue backpack heavy with books he could not read. Sansan kissed him at the door, helped him remove the backpack and poured him a bowl of sweet bean porridge. After his snack, he bent over his reader at the kitchen table. He breathed with effort, sounding out each English word so slowly that Ming did not see how he could remember what he had read.

The sight of him lit a fear in Ming's mind. "If you pay him less attention, he might want to stay in school instead of flying home to you," he told Sansan.

She said, "You don't know about children."

"I was not so coddled by my mother."

"The other children make fun of him."

Ming frowned. He reread the teacher's letter. That evening, when Charles had finished his bath and climbed into Ming and Sansan's bed for his nighttime ritual, Ming told his son there would be no bedtime story.

Charles sat perfectly still. "No story?"

"Daddy thinks we should speak English for a while," Sansan explained.

Ming watched his son's face. Recently, Charles had developed an expression of careful solitude. "I can read to you from your schoolbook," Ming said.

Charles shook his head.

"Do you understand why you need to learn English?" Ming asked.

Charles nodded. In the next few months, he gradually stopped speaking Chinese. Since they did not test him, Ming never knew how long it took for all of those words to be forgotten.

MANY other things passed out of memory without their noticing. Sansan stopped reading her Chinese classics and romances. When they'd first moved to Mercy Lake, she had reread them until their bindings buckled, shredded, and fell off. She had even tried to get Ming to skim the books, so she would have someone to talk to, but Ming was busy at work. Then came Charles's letter from Mrs. Carlsen. Eventually, the tales were pushed into a smaller and smaller part of her mind, until the characters and stories only came up now and then, usually in her dreams, and when they did, she said to Ming, they seemed almost quaint, exotic. The novels found their way onto a shelf, in the basement, where they stood next to a red-bound history text that Ming and Sansan had kept in order to remind themselves of their culture and the importance of their race.

Instead of reading, Sansan practiced her English by watching television. She also took good care of Ming and Charles. She laundered Ming's new work clothes: permanent-press shirts with plastic tabs inserted in the stiff, pointed collars; bright, wide ties. Ming needed to dress well, because he had found a second calling as a salesman. He had discovered that clients were comforted by his appearance and his accent, which went together, in some way, with his efficiency and mechanical know-how. He began persuading them to buy larger, more expensive machines. He asked for and received a commission for each machine he sold. These extra monies, he and Sansan agreed, would go into a savings account for Charles's education at the University of Iowa.

In the kitchen, Sansan learned to cook with canned and frozen foods. She made cream of tomato soup for lunch, and stored envelopes of onion soup mix for meat loaf or quick onion dip. More often as Ming's career improved, Sansan consulted the Betty Crocker cookbook and made something for him to bring to an office party or to entertain a coworker at home. She kept a filebox listing everything she made, with annotations reminding her which dishes the Americans liked and didn't like.

She bought air freshener in a plastic daisy, and a jello mold shaped like a fish. They taught Charles to use a knife and fork, and they ate their meals off brittle plastic plates that they had chosen at the discount store: bright, hard disks, flat and cheerful, the color of candy: scarlet, lime green, yellow, and white.

THEY forgot some things deliberately; they wanted to forget. Ming won a trip for two to Chicago, based on his annual sales, and he did not protest when Sansan bought an expensive new suitcase rather than open her old yellow carpetbag and confront the six white rice bowls. At work, Ming avoided one well-meaning coworker who had once asked, "What was it like in China? It must be different from here." How could he answer that question without remembering the smell of fresh rolls sold on the street, or the scent of his grandfather's pipe?

Ming forgot the delicate taste of his grandfather's favorite fruit, the yellow watermelon. He forgot his grandfather's hopes that he might study hard and rebuild China. He forgot the fact that he had once desired to earn a Ph.D., to work in a laboratory, to discover great things and add to the body of humanity's scientific knowledge.

He replaced such useless memories with thoughts of Charles. It was for Charles that Ming had taken his job in Iowa and bought his house, because he had believed, since Charles was born, that he could make a new life in America.

He struggled through clumsy conversations at the office and employee "happy hours," practicing his English. For Charles, he read the local newspaper and mowed the lawn. With Charles in mind, he struggled out of bed on winter mornings, fighting sleepiness and persistent dreams. He maintained the new Chevrolet sedan—changed the oil, followed the tune-up dates, and kept good records of all repairs.

He labored on the yard. They had moved into a neighborhood so new that at certain times the air was redolent of cow, and Ming would dream that he was being watched by large, calm eyes, and that their house had been surrounded by those strange and fragrant animals. The soil itself seemed exotic to Ming; it looked so coarse, so rich and reddish-purple—not exhausted by three thousand years of farming, like the Chinese earth, but exuberant and wild. Ming could sense the rolling fields that pressed upon their house. Mutinous seeds opposed the lawn: tall leaves of pale new wheat, foamy milkweed, Queen Anne's lace. He fussed over his spears of frail bluegrass. In the autumn he reseeded and raked, pruned back the shrubs, hid San-san's yellow rosebush under its protective cone; but in the spring, when the melting snow lay bare his lawn, he watched and held his breath. He did not quite trust the land. He did not know what he might find. On warm spring nights, he lay awake and listened to a distant hum amidst the silence; it might have been the wind over ten thousand acres of fields, or the hatching of a thousand insects. He did not want to miss these changes. He wanted nothing taking place behind his back.

CHARLES'S English did improve. To Ming's surprise, he read all the time: after school, in front of the television, on

Saturday mornings, over meals, and even, his teachers told Ming and Sansan, during recess. In fifth grade, his teachers were pleased. In sixth grade, they were excited, and by the time he entered seventh grade, his level of achievement was, they said, phenomenal.

Even more, the teachers said, he seemed to find a pure pleasure in learning—an almost obsessive pleasure. He once failed to hear a fire drill bell while reading a biography of Thomas Paine. He wrote his papers, they said, with such articulate and righteous passion that his assignments more than compensated for his lack of class participation. He was drawn to the humanities and he seemed to be developing a passion for examining the past; he possessed a truly unusual mind.

Why the humanities? Ming wondered. What intricate foldings lay behind his son's quiet face; what opinions had formed beneath his stiff-mown hair? The autumn of Charles's eighth-grade year, Ming bought him a wooden desk and a sturdy lamp with a metal shade. He adjusted his chair and bolted a steel pencil sharpener into the wall. Then he and Sansan drove to the discount store and heaped a shopping cart with blue spiral notebooks (his favorite color) as well as blue pencils, a blue cloth-covered binder, and an enormous blue eraser. Charles brought these things to school in his backpack, and after that, Ming glimpsed them only now and then, evidence of his son's mysterious passions.

One winter evening, while Charles was helping his mother set the dining room table, Ming said, "I think I understand your interest in history. I used to like to read the history of science. I used to love science." He allowed his mind a glimpse—only a glimpse—into the basement, through the sliding panel of his desk, at the *Handbook of Chemistry and Physics*. "Do you like science?"

Charles looked up, the silverware clutched in his hand. "Not really," he said quickly. "But in history, I learned about trains." He began to talk about the European and American-born pioneers who had settled the land and made it into fields and towns. Ming watched him gesture, still holding their three forks in one brown hand, his wrists grown out of his last year's shirtsleeves. He described how the use of trains had sped the populating of the West, and how the transcontinental railroad had been built by Chinese immigrants. Then, to Ming's dismay, he asked, "Why was China so poor that people had to come to the U.S. and work on the railroads?"

Ming did not know how to tackle this enormous question. "Well," he said finally, "I'm not certain of that, but the country has always been poor."

"Why is that? Did you learn about it when you were in school?"

"We studied history."

"Did you like history?"

Ming stood and thought for a moment. "To tell you the truth," he said, "I can't remember."

That careful, lonely look came into Charles's face. He went into the kitchen and left Ming standing at the table, regretting how he had ended the conversation. He found himself envying the easy way that Charles reached for the past. How could he explain to his son that the past was his enemy? That his memories dogged him, filled his thoughts and plans with silt? They rose up in his dreams, the way that in the spring the Mercy Lake flooded through its margins, leaving the fishing huts surrounded by water.

H E could not forget the colors of the Beijing sky. At night, in bed, he remembered the burning smell on winter nights from the thousand coal fires that burned in kitchens and under old-fashioned brick beds, the thousand pale streams of smoke that rose into the darkness. He recalled the grit of the spring dust storms catching in his throat, and the loose slat on the wall of the noodle-making shop that had enabled him to peer inside at the man who thinned the noodles by hand.

Ming could not forget one warm and beautiful summer evening in 1932, when he had helped his Uncle Lu pack up his belongings. The family was leaving Beijing, for what they thought would be only a few years, the duration of the war. Uncle Lu, his father's youngest brother, had never taken a real job but had remained in the family house, supported by his brothers and sisters, like an invalid, long after his beard indicated that he should have had a family of his own. As far as Ming could recall, his Uncle Lu was only interested in the practice of calligraphy. He had no other desires, it seemed, but to sit before a well-lit table, the brush upright in his hand, a gentle hand unfit for more practical tasks. That night, when they were not half finished, his uncle had sat down at his desk, helplessly, and looked about his little room, with tears rolling down his cheeks. Ming had turned away in embarassment and hurried to pack the precious brushes and rolls of soft, white paper—the only things Uncle Lu wanted brought with him.

Where had those brushes and papers gone? What had become of the scrolls that Lu had painted and saved, so carefully? Nothing remained except Ming's recollection of them. Charles had never even seen a photograph of his great uncle. Like everyone else, Lu had died. He had suffered a stroke the night after the family left Beijing, the first casualty in a long line of lost and missing. Only a few cousins were living now, and they were scattered. Any photographs had been lost. Sometimes, Ming wondered if it were possible—that of the over two dozen members of that household everyone was scattered and gone. He could not believe that of the grandparents, uncles and aunts, cousins, and so many others, that this family had dwindled into the slender thread of his own memory.

BY the time Charles entered high school he had impressed his teachers as a young man with a singular determination and potential. They said he needed to relax more, that was all. They said he seemed "like a fish out of water" during lunch period. Academically, he continued to excel. In his World History class, he developed an interest in World War II and, in particular, the Pacific theater.

One spring night Ming went to Charles's room to ask his son if he wanted a bowl of sweet bean porridge. He trudged down the hall, with no particular expectation, but was surprised to find his son's door closed. He stood dumbly for a moment and then, without thinking, he put his hand on the knob. The door was locked.

He knocked, foolishly, a little angry. After a moment, he heard the creak of a mattress, three steps toward the door. The lock clicked open.

"Charles?"

They were of a height, he noticed. Charles was so young that even when weary, he looked fresh. Ming observed his son, in whose narrow face he recognized his own; he noted the smooth, brown skin Charles had inherited from Sansan. What did he have to be weary about? "What are you doing?" Ming asked, despite the fact that he could see the books and papers strewn over the bed.

"What do you mean?"

Ming retreated. "I came up to see if you would like some *lu dou tang*."

"No, not right now, thanks." With such politeness Ming was thus rebuffed. Charles closed the door in his face and Ming stood there, blank for a moment. Then he turned and went back to the kitchen. Halfway down the hall he heard the lock click shut again.

That night, his dreams kept bringing him down the hallway, and he stood once again before his son's locked door. The next day he could not concentrate at work. The image of the door disturbed him, as if Charles had access to another world inside that room, as if he might disappear at will, might float from their second-story windows and vanish into the shimmering, yellow Iowa light.

He used a Phillips screwdriver to take apart the door-knobs and disable the locks on Charles's bedroom, the bathrooms, and the upstairs closets. Charles said nothing to him. But later Ming heard him ask his mother, "What did Dad do to my lock?" Ming caught these words one morning on his way out and paused to listen. "That's all right," Sansan said. Ming heard the squeak of a kiss. "Things get old sometimes. Don't tell Daddy—you'll make him feel bad."

Later he attempted to defend himself. A family, he told Sansan, should need no windows and no doors. In China there had been no locks on children's rooms. True, they had come to America—but even in this country, what obedient child would *need* to lock his parents from his room? "He doesn't respect me," Ming insisted.

"Of course he does."

"He's my son—I can tell from his voice, the shape of his face. But sometimes I wonder if he's my son!"

"Hush," said Sansan. She cocked her head, gesturing toward Charles's room. They both listened, but the house was absolutely quiet. The comforting odor of fried rice lingered in the air. Ming listened more closely. Beyond the house, from the land, he could hear the distant hum of early spring.

DESPITE their efforts, they could not forget their language, the musical pitch of Mandarin tones, the shapes of phrases. Over and over, they reached for certain words that had no equivalents in English. Sansan could find no substitute for the word *yiwei*, which meant that a person "had once assumed, but incorrectly." And no matter how much he drilled himself, Ming could not instinctively convert the measure *wan* to "ten thousand," rather than "a thousand."

In English, Sansan seemed to hide from her more complicated thoughts. "So much is missing," she told Ming. Her English world was limited to the clipped and casual rhythm of daily plans. "Put on your tie." "Did you turn on the rice?" "Be home by five o'clock."

Later that spring, there came a rainy evening when Charles looked up from his book and said, "Tomorrow I can't be home until ten."

"Is there a school event of yours that we should go to?" Ming asked.

"No." Charles flipped his book out of its jacket and folded it back. "It's college night," he said, finally. "The guidance counselor is ordering pizza. Then a man is coming to talk to us about college."

Ming nudged Sansan. "We like you to come home for dinner," Sansan said. "We don't get to see you otherwise."

Charles moved his lips for a moment, then looked up at them. "Sometime I'll have to go to college," he said. Then he stopped.

Ming jumped in. "We've been saving for you to go to college! I wanted to go to college, myself. You know that!"

Hunger

His voice cracked. He frowned at Sansan. "Why are you looking at me like that?"

She said, "Let's talk about this later."

A painful knot, the size of a cherry stone, formed inside Ming's throat and stayed there. Sansan turned on the television. Neither spoke until Charles had gone back to his room. Then they went to their own bedroom and undressed in silence.

In bed, in the dark, Sansan turned to him. "It's funny," she said. "I am very proud of Charles. But lately, I've been thinking it's not enough."

Ming swallowed and nodded in the dark.

"Do you remember the second Taipei flood?" she asked, cautiously, in Mandarin this time.

Ming muttered, "Maybe—not too well. Maybe you should remind me."

Her words, in Mandarin, came slowly at first and then more easily, low and wondering, as if she were marveling at her ability to speak. Her murmuring voice flowed with the steady drumming of the storm.

"Remember how poor we were? We were so poor that we could only afford one vegetable with the rice. We had to live with my mother's old Aunt Green Blossom in her flat over that restaurant, the Drunken Moon. On the day of the storm, the restaurant was serving flounder. A big catch must have just come in. When you got home for lunch, the scent of ginger and garlic sprouts, with oil, had soaked into our room."

He knew she spoke to comfort him, but his eyes had filled with tears.

"The smell from the restaurant made us quarrel with each other," she said. "That afternoon, the rains began; we holed ourselves inside and watched the commotion from the window. It rained until the streets were rivers. And you had a wonderful idea."

He smiled then. "It wasn't wonderful; it was scientific

logic. The Drunken Moon was only one step up."

"We waited; we watched the water rise, then trickle over the step. All the customers left. The neighborhood was as flooded as a rice paddy. And then you went downstairs and asked them if they needed a dry place to store their food!" She laughed. "How well we ate that night!"

Ming looked at his wife. He could barely see her profile in the glow from their bedside clock. She lay on her back now, gazing at the ceiling. "Lately," she said, "I've been dreaming about that meal. Over and over. And I wonder why the food we eat now doesn't taste as good."

THEIR memories seeped under the doors and sifted through the keyhole. They had taken root in the earth itself, as tough and stubborn as the weeds in the garden. It seemed to Ming that after seven years in Mercy Lake, the world of his past had grown every day larger and more vivid until it pressed against his mind, beautiful and shining. And he wondered if perhaps this world had pushed his own son out of his house—if they had lost their son because of their stubborn inability to forget.

One evening he came home early. Sansan had gone to the library. In the mailbox was a letter from the guidance counselor at Charles's high school; he wanted to congratulate Charles's parents for his high test scores, and he was certain that their son would be an excellent student at the prestigious East Coast college that he had applied to, early admission. Ming read this letter; he pushed his glasses up his nose, and read it again, the paper weightless in his hands.

Ming went to his son's room. Everything lay neatly under the lamplight: the desk, the piles of books, the plain blue bedspread. Charles sat at his desk, surrounded by piles of homework. A college brochure lay open before him.

"The best state school is only an hour away," Ming said.

Charles took a deep breath. "But I don't want to go to the state school," he said.

This fact drowned out all sound for a moment, but when Ming's thoughts cleared he grew aware that Charles was still talking. Charles was saying, Did they realize how little he knew about the world? He needed to know what the world was like, the world outside of their house, outside of Iowa, so that for the rest of his life he would not remain entirely lost.

"Why didn't you tell me?" Ming asked.

"I knew you didn't want me to leave."

"Why do you want to leave, then?"

Charles looked at him. "Because I know I have to go," he said.

Ming said nothing. Charles turned his attention to his brochure. After a few minutes Ming realized that his son had ended the conversation. He stood, bewildered, and walked out, closing the door behind him. When he reached the foot of the stairs, he stopped and glanced again at the closed door.

AFTER this, it seemed to Ming that the very passage of days imprisoned him. Each morning, alone in the small bathroom, he cleared his throat and blew his nose—he had developed an allergy to ragweed over the years. His cough rang off the tiles. In the kitchen, his tea steamed sour against his upper lip. He left the house, and climbed into the Chevrolet. These habits built around him a dark and airless riddle. Charles was a part of it; even Sansan was a part of it.

On the day after they learned that Charles had been accepted early to Harvard, Sansan cooked a celebratory dinner. Afterward, they waited all evening for their son to go upstairs, their eyes bright and voices low, deliberate, and harsh. Ming tidied the messy coffee table with shaking hands. Sansan folded laundry, gripping the center of the sheets between her teeth. Charles vanished off to bed, as if he could smell the sulfur in the air. He stepped out of the room so quietly they would never have noticed if they had not been waiting.

Later, they turned off the television and faced each other. The air between them quivered as if they had been waiting to make love.

Sansan shrugged. "What did you expect?" she asked. "Sons in this country leave their parents and make their own homes, with their women." Her voice was tense, accusatory.

Ming took a sharp breath. "And that is all you have to say?"

"Isn't this what you wanted for him? That he should become like them?" Her voice grew higher. "No, I have nothing else to say."

"What *I* wanted?" Ming's voice rose. "So this is all my fault?"

"It is what you wanted! It was your idea to get a job here, in the middle of nowhere—your idea!"

"It's your fault as much as mine!"

She was standing before him, her knees bent and both feet planted, her face distorted, shouting suddenly, "You're lying!" Then, without taking her eyes from him, she moved backward, toward the dishrack. She reached blindly for a brittle, plastic plate, raised it slowly into the air, as if she were casting a spell, then flung it against the kitchen floor.

For a moment Ming stood, arrested by the sight of the red disk hurtling downward, surprised to see it breaking into pieces against the floor. He had not known such goods could shatter. Then he walked slowly to the cabinet, his heavy fingers tingling at his sides.

Hunger

They broke every plate on the shelf, plus the china pencil holder and the good teapot. Sansan stood with knees bent and both feet planted, near the dishrack, jerking her arm downward to emphasize a point, tears flying as she shook her head from side to side. She shouted, *"You are the cause of this! You have ruined me! You have trapped me into this life!"* "I should go downstairs and get those rice bowls!" Ming threatened. "Go ahead!" she shouted. "Why did we save them, anyway?" The words flew from their mouths, whirled through the kitchen. Colorful disks flew through the air, cracked and bounced against the walls, the chairs, the cabinets.

When they had finished, they stood transfixed, breathing hard, admiring their handiwork. The broken pieces made a bright mosaic on the floor.

A certain quality to the silence made them both look up.

The kitchen door had somehow been left open. There stood Charles in his pajamas, squinting in the light. He whispered, "I wish you would be happy for me."

In that moment, Ming understood that Charles was indeed his son. There was no question about it. The resemblance wasn't in the shape of his face. It was in his look of sorrow.

After Charles left the room, they turned once more toward each other. Sansan's face was rigid and blank. What had happened to them? Ming wondered. What would happen? He had no one to ask—no friends, no parents—no one who could have understood the language of his thoughts.

Now Sansan stood by the back door, holding her jacket. "I want to go back," she said. Her voice was shaking. "Why did you have to bring me here?"

She turned and quietly left the house, clicking the door shut behind her. Ming stood inside. He made out her shape in the dim garage as she got into the Chevrolet, backed it out in one quick motion, and drove west, toward the highway.

F O R an hour, he sat at the kitchen table. He had switched off the lights, and the blackness soothed his mind. He fixed his gaze upon the square of faint streetlight that lay upon the counter.

He was alone. What kind of cruelty had held him back from saying what she most desired to hear? That he needed her. That even with Charles gone, they would endure.

The Chevrolet moved like a comet in his mind. Sansan, never a confident driver, veering left onto Polk Avenue. The neighborhood houses prim on either side of her, reflecting the pale car in their dark windows. She would list over the center line and then correct herself. She would enter the freeway, careening down the empty entrance ramp; she would turn north, away from the new commercial area, and toward the country roads that stretched among the winter fields, the dried-up stalks of corn, the earth rich and softly dark, scattered with snow and bits of wheat and chaff from the harvest. He knew his wife. For a long time, he had suspected that a part of her longed simply to disappear into those fields. The car would jounce a bit as she turned onto the gravel, then into the simplest two-tire track in the dirt. And there she might sit amidst the harvested soy beans, surrounded by silence, resting. Why did so many farmers grow soy beans? Ming wondered. No one in a hundred miles would dream of buying soy sauce. He imagined the local people were secure in their desires for steak and milk, protected by their barns, their tractors, and their slumbering cows.

Would she leave him? Perhaps she would leave, now that they had glimpsed their fate. Perhaps she would be able to forget—free and clear, wiped clean at last. Ming imagined her leaving the dirt roads and heading across the local highway to join the night traffic on the interstate, merging silently into the stream of traffic.

But even as he envisioned this, he knew it would not happen. Sansan had nowhere else to go. Nothing remained of the stories and meals and people they'd known, nothing but what they remembered. Their world lived in them, and they would be the end of it. They had no solace, and no burden, but each other.

THE next morning, as he warmed up the car, he stooped to examine the tires. He found mud and grains of yellow wheat embedded deep into the treads.

THE EVE OF THE
SPIRIT FESTIVAL

AFTER THE BUDDHIST CEREMONY, WHEN our mother's spirit had been chanted to a safe passage and her body cremated, Emily and I sat silently on our living room carpet. She held me in her arms; her long hair stuck to our wet faces. We sat as stiffly as temple gods except for the angry thump of my sister's heart against my cheek.

Finally she spoke. "It's Baba's fault," she said. "The American doctors would have fixed her."

I was six years old—I only knew that our father and mother had decided against an operation. And I had privately agreed, imagining the doctors tearing a hole in her body. As I thought of this, I felt a sudden sob pass through me.

"Don't cry, Baby," Emily whispered. "You're okay." I felt my tears dry to salt, my throat lock shut.

Then our father walked into the room.

He and Emily had grown close in the past few months. Emily was eleven, old enough to come along on his trips to the hospital. I had often stood in the neighbor's window and watched them leave for visiting hours, Emily's mittened hand tucked into his.

But now my sister refused to acknowledge him. She pushed the back of my head to turn me away from him also.

"First daughter—" he began.

"Go away, Baba," Emily said. Her voice shook. The evening sun glowed garnet red through the dark tent of her hair.

"You told me she would get better," I heard her say. "Now you're burning paper money for her ghost. What good will that do?"

"I am sorry," Baba said.

"I don't care."

Her voice burned. I squirmed beneath her hand, but she wouldn't let me look. It was something between her and Baba. I watched his black wingtip shoes retreat to the door. When he had gone, Emily let go of me. I sat up and looked at her; something had changed. Not in the lovely outlines of her face—our mother's face—but in her eyes, shadow-black, lost in unforgiveness.

THEY say the dead return to us. But we never saw our mother again, though we kept a kind of emptiness waiting in case she might come back. I listened always, seeking her voice, the lost thread of a conversation I'd been too young to have with her. I did not dare mention her to Emily. Since I could remember, my sister had kept her most powerful feelings private, sealed away. She rarely mentioned our mother, and soon my memories faded. I could not picture her. I saw only Emily's angry face, the late sun streaking red through her dark hair.

After the traditional forty-nine day mourning period, Baba did not set foot in the Buddhist temple. It was as if he had listened to Emily: what good did it do? Instead he focused on earthly ambitions, his research at the lab.

At that time he aspired beyond the position of lab instructor to the rank of associate professor, and he often invited his American colleagues over for "drinks." Emily and I were recruited to help with the preparations and serving. As we went about our tasks, we would sometimes catch a glimpse of our father, standing in the corner, watching the American men and studying to become one.

But he couldn't get it right—our parties had an air of cultural confusion. We served potato chips on laquered trays; Chinese landscapes bumped against watercolors of the Statue of Liberty, the Empire State Building.

Nor were Emily or I capable of helping him. I was still a child, and Emily said she did not care. Since my mother's death, she had rejected anything he held dear. She refused to study chemistry and spoke in American slang. Her rebellion puzzled me, it seemed so vehement and so arbitrary.

Now she stalked through the living room, platform shoes thudding on the carpet. "I hate this," she said, fiercely ripping another rag from a pair of old pajama bottoms. "Entertaining these jerks is a waste of time."

Some chemists from Texas were visiting his department and he had invited them over for cocktails.

"I can finish it," I said. "You just need to do the parts I can't reach."

"It's not the dusting," she said. "It's the way he acts around them. 'Herro, herro! Hi Blad, hi Warry! Let me take your coat! Howsa Giants game?'" she mimicked, in a voice that made me wince, a voice alive with cruelty and pain. "If he were smart he wouldn't invite people over on football afternoons in the first place."

"What do you mean?" I asked, startled. Brad Delmonte

was our father's boss. I had noticed Baba reading the sports pages that morning—something he rarely did.

"Oh, forget it," Emily said. I felt as if she and I were utterly separate. Then she smiled. "You've got oil on your glasses, Claudia."

Baba walked in carrying two bottles of wine. "They should arrive in half an hour," he said, looking at his watch. "They won't be early. Americans are never early."

Emily looked away. "I'm going to Jodie's house," she said.

Baba frowned and straightened his tie. "I want you to stay while they're here. We might need something from the kitchen."

"Claudia can get it for them."

"She's barely tall enough to reach the cabinets."

Emily stood and clenched her dustcloth. "I don't care," she said. "I hate meeting the people you have over."

"They're successful American scientists. You'd be better off with them instead of running around with your teenage friends, these sloppy kids, these rich white kids who dress like beggars."

"You're nuts, Dad," Emily said—she had begun addressing him the way an American child does. "You're nuts if you think these bosses of yours are ever going to do anything for you or any of us." And she threw her dustcloth, hard, into our New York Giants wastebasket.

"Speak to me with respect."

"You don't deserve it!"

"You are staying in this apartment! That is an order!"

"I wish you'd died instead of Mama!" Emily cried. She darted past our father, her long braid flying behind her. He stared at her, his expression oddly slack, the way it had been in the weeks after the funeral. He stepped toward her, reached hesitantly at her flying braid, but she turned and saw him, cried out as if he had struck her, and ran out of the room. His hands dropped to his sides.

Emily refused to leave our bedroom. Otherwise that party was like so many others. The guests arrived late and left early. They talked about buying new cars and the Dallas Cowboys. I served pretzels and salted nuts.

Baba walked around emptying ashtrays and refilling drinks. I noticed that the other men also wore vests and ties, but that the uniform looked somehow different on my slighter, darker father.

"Cute little daughter you have there," said Baba's boss. He was a large bearded smoker with a sandy voice. He didn't bend down to look at me or the ashtray that I raised toward his big square hand.

I went into our room and found Emily sitting on one of our unmade twin beds. It was dusk. Through the window I could see that the dull winter sun had almost disappeared. I sat next to her on the bed. Until that day, I think, it was Emily who took care of me and not the other way around.

After a minute, she spoke. "I'm going to leave," she said. "As soon as I turn eighteen, I'm going to leave home and never come back!" She burst into tears. I reached for her shoulder but her thin, heaving body frightened me. She seemed too grown up to be comforted. I thought about the breasts swelling beneath her sweater. Her body had become a foreign place.

PERHAPS Emily had warned me that she would someday leave in order to start me off on my own. I found myself avoiding her, as though her impending desertion would matter less if I deserted her first. I discovered a place to hide while she and my father fought, in the living room behind a painted screen. I would read a novel or look out the window. Sometimes they forgot about me—from the next room I would hear one of them break off an argument and say, "Where did Claudia go?" "I don't know," the other would reply. After a silence, they would start again.

One of these fights stands out in my memory. I must have been ten or eleven years old. It was the fourteenth day of the seventh lunar month: the eve of Guijie, the Chinese Spirit Festival, when the living are required to appease and provide for the ghosts of their ancestors. To the believing, the earth was thick with gathering spirits; it was safest to stay indoors and burn incense.

I seldom thought about the Chinese calendar, but every year on Guijie I wondered about my mother's ghost. Where was it? Would it still recognize me? How would I know when I saw it? I wanted to ask Baba, but I didn't dare. Baba had an odd attitude toward Guijie. On one hand, he had eschewed all Chinese customs since my mother's death. He was a scientist, he said; he scorned the traditional tales of unsatisfied spirits roaming the earth.

But I cannot remember a time when I was not made aware, in some way, of Guijie's fluctuating lunar date. That year the eve of the Spirit Festival fell on a Thursday, usually his night out with the men from his department. Emily and I waited for him to leave but he sat on the couch, calmly reading the *New York Times*.

I finished drying the dishes. Emily began to fidget. She had a date that night and had counted on my father's absence. She spent half an hour washing and combing her hair, trying to make up her mind. Finally she asked me to give her a trim. I knew she'd decided to go out.

"Just a little," she said. "The ends are scraggly." We spread some newspapers on the living room floor. Emily stood in the middle of the papers with her hair combed down her back, thick and glossy, black as ink. It hadn't really been cut since she was born. Since my mother's death I had taken over the task of giving it a periodic touch-up.

I hovered behind her with the shears, searching for the scraggly ends, but there were none.

My father looked up from his newspaper. "What are you doing that for? You can't go out tonight," he said.

"I have a date!"

My father put down his newspaper. I threw the shears onto a chair and fled to my refuge behind the screen.

Through a slit over the hinge I caught a glimpse of Emily near the foyer, slender in her denim jacket, her black hair flooding down her back, her delicate features contorted with anger. My father's hair was disheveled, his hands clenched at his sides. The newspapers had scattered over the floor.

"Dressing up in boys' clothes, with paint on your face—"

"This is nothing! My going out on a few dates is nothing! You don't know what you're talking about!"

"Don't shout." My father shook his finger. "The neighbors will hear you."

"Goddammit, Dad!" Her voice rose to a shriek. She stamped her feet to make the most noise possible.

"What happened to you?" he cried. "You used to be so much like her. Look at you—"

Though I'd covered my ears I could hear my sister's wail echo off the walls. The door slammed, and her footfalls vanished down the stairs.

Things were quiet for a minute. Then I heard my father walk toward my corner. My heart thumped with fear—usually he let me alone. I had to look up when I heard him move the screen away. He knelt down next to me. His hair was streaked with gray, and his glasses needed cleaning.

"What are you doing?" he asked.

I shook my head, nothing.

After a minute I asked him, "Is Guijie why you didn't go play bridge tonight, Baba?"

"No, Claudia," he said. He always called me by my American name. This formality, I thought, was an indication of how distant he felt from me. "I stopped playing bridge last week."

"Why?" We both looked toward the window, where beyond our reflections the Hudson River flowed.

"It's not important," he said.

"Okay."

But he didn't leave. "I'm getting old," he said after a moment. "Someone ten years younger was just promoted over me. I'm not going to try to keep up with them anymore."

It was the closest he had ever come to confiding in me. After a few more minutes he stood up and went into the kitchen. The newspapers rustled under his feet. For almost half an hour I heard him fumbling through the kitchen cabinets, looking for something he'd probably put there years ago. Eventually he came out, carrying a small brass urn and some matches. When Emily returned home after midnight, the apartment still smelled of the incense he had burned to protect her while she was gone.

I TRIED to be a good daughter. I stayed in every night and wore no make-up, I studied hard and got all A's, I did not leave home but went to college at NYU, right down the street. Jealously I guarded my small allotment of praise, clutching it like a pocket of precious stones. Emily snuck out of the apartment late at night; she wore high-heeled sandals with patched blue jeans; she twisted her long hair into graceful, complex loops and braids that belied respectability. She smelled of lipstick and perfume. Nothing I could ever achieve would equal my sister's misbehavior.

When Emily turned eighteen and did leave home, a part of my father disappeared. I wondered sometimes: where did it go? Did she take it with her? What secret charm had she carried with her as she vanished down the tunnel to the jet that would take her to college in California, steadily and without looking back, while my father and I watched silently from the window at the gate? The apartment afterwards became quite still—it was only the two of us, mourning and dreaming through pale-blue winter afternoons and silent evenings.

Emily called me, usually late at night after my father had gone to sleep. She sent me pictures of herself and people I didn't know, smiling on the sunny Berkeley campus. Sometimes after my father and I ate our simple meals or TV dinners I would go into our old room, where I had kept both of our twin beds, and take out Emily's pictures, trying to imagine what she must have been feeling, studying her expression and her swinging hair. But I always stared the longest at a postcard she'd sent me one winter break from northern New Mexico, a professional photo of a powerful, vast blue sky over faraway pink and sandy-beige mesas. The clarity and cleanness fascinated me. In a place like that, I thought, there would be nothing to search for, no reason to hide.

After college she went to work at a bank in San Francisco. I saw her once when she flew to Manhattan on business. She skipped a meeting to have lunch with me. She wore an elegant gray suit and had pinned up her hair.

"How's Dad?" she asked. I looked around, slightly alarmed. We were sitting in a bistro on the East Side, but I somehow thought he might overhear us.

"He's okay," I said. "We don't talk very much. Why don't you come home and see him?"

Emily stared at her water glass. "I don't think so."

"He misses you."

"I know. I don't want to hear about it."

"You hardly ever call him."

"There's nothing we can talk about. Don't tell him you saw me, promise?"

"Okay."

During my junior year at NYU, my father suffered a stroke. He was fifty-nine years old, and he was still working as a lab instructor in the chemistry department. One evening in early fall I came home from a class and found him on the floor, near the kitchen telephone. He was wearing his usual vest and tie. I called the hospital and sat down next to him. His wire-rimmed glasses lay on the floor a foot away. One-half of his face was frozen, the other half lined with sudden age and pain.

"They said they'll be right here," I said. "It won't be very long." I couldn't tell how much he understood. I smoothed his vest and straightened his tie. I folded his glasses. I knew he wouldn't like it if the ambulance workers saw him in a state of dishevelment. "I'm sure they'll be here soon," I said.

We waited. Then I noticed he was trying to tell me something. A line of spittle ran from the left side of his mouth. I leaned closer. After a while I made out his words: "Tell Emily," he said.

The ambulance arrived as I picked up the telephone to call California. That evening, at the hospital, what was remaining of my father left the earth.

EMILY insisted that we not hold a Buddhist cremation ceremony. "I never want to think about that stuff again," she said. "Plus, all of his friends are Americans. I don't know who would come, except for us." She had reached New York the morning after his death. Her eyes were vague and her fingernails bitten down.

On the third day we scattered his ashes in the river. Afterward we held a small memorial service for his friends from work. We didn't talk much as we straightened the living room and dusted the furniture. It took almost three hours. The place was a mess. We hadn't had a party in years.

It was a warm cloudy afternoon, and the Hudson looked dull and sluggish from the living room window. I noticed that although she had not wanted a Buddhist ceremony, Emily had dressed in black and white according to Chinese mourning custom. I had asked the department secretary to put up a sign on the bulletin board. Eleven people came; they drank five bottles of wine. Two of his Chinese students stood in the corner, eating cheese and crackers.

Brad Delmonte, paunchy and no longer smoking, attached himself to Emily. "I remember you when you were just a little girl," I heard him say as I walked by with the extra crackers.

"I don't remember you," she said.

"You're still a cute little thing." She bumped his arm, and he spilled his drink.

Afterward we sat on the couch and surveyed the cluttered coffee table. It was past seven but we didn't talk about dinner.

"I'm glad they came," I said.

"I hate them." Emily looked at her fingernails. "I don't know whom I hate more: them, or him—for taking it."

"It doesn't matter anymore," I said.

"I suppose."

We watched the room grow dark.

"Do you know what?" Emily said. "It's the eve of the fifteenth day of the seventh lunar month."

"How do you know?" During college I had grown completely unaware of the lunar calendar.

"One of those chemistry nerds from Taiwan told me this afternoon."

I wanted to laugh, but instead I felt myself make a strange whimpering sound, squeezed out from my tight and hollow chest.

"Remember the time Dad and I had that big fight?" she said. "You know that now, in my grown-up life, I don't fight with anyone? I never had problems with anybody except him."

"No one cared about you as much as he did," I said.

"I don't want to hear about it." She twisted the end of her long braid. "He was a pain, and you know it. He got so strict after Mama died. It wasn't all my fault."

"I'm sorry," I said. But I was so angry with her that I felt my face turn red, my cheeks tingle in the dark. She'd considered our father a nerd as well, had squandered his love with such thoughtlessness that I could scarcely breathe to think about it. It seemed impossibly unfair that she had memories of my mother as well. Carefully I waited for my feelings to go away. Emily, I thought, was all I had.

But as I sat, a vision distilled before my eyes: the soft baked shades, the great blue sky of New Mexico. I realized that after graduation I could go wherever I wanted. A rusty door swung open and filled my mind with sweet freedom, fearful coolness.

"Let's do something," I said.

"What do you mean?"

"I want to do something."

"What did we used to do?" Emily looked down at the lock of hair in her hand. "Wait, I know."

We found newspapers and spread them on the floor. We turned on the lamps and moved the coffee table out of the way, brought the wineglasses to the sink. Emily went to the bathroom, and I searched for the shears a long time before I found them in the kitchen. I glimpsed the incense urn in a cabinet and quickly shut the door. When I returned to the living room it smelled of shampoo. Emily stood in the middle of the papers with her wet hair down her back, staring at herself in the reflection from the window. The lamplight cast circles under her eyes.

"I had a dream last night," she said. "I was walking down the street. I felt a tug. He was trying to reach me, trying to pull my hair."

"Just a trim?" I asked.

"No," she said. "Why don't you cut it."

"What do you mean?" I snipped a two-inch lock off the side.

Emily looked down at the hair on the newspapers. "I'm serious," she said. "Cut my hair. I want to see two feet of hair on the floor."

"Emily, you don't know what you're saying," I said. But a pleasurable, weightless feeling had come over me. I placed the scissors at the nape of her neck. "How about it?" I asked, and my voice sounded low and odd.

"*I don't care.*" An echo of the past. I cut. The shears went *snack*. A long black lock of hair hit the newspapers by my feet.

The Chinese say that our hair and our bodies are given to us from our ancestors, gifts that should not be tampered with. My mother herself had never done this. But after the first few moments I enjoyed myself, pressing the thick black locks through the shears, heavy against my thumb. Emily's hair slipped to the floor around us, rich and beautiful, lying in long graceful arcs over my shoes. She stood perfectly still, staring out the window. The Hudson River flowed behind our reflections, bearing my father's ashes through the night.

When I was finished, the back of her neck gleamed clean and white under a precise shining cap. "You missed your calling," Emily said. "You want me to do yours?"

My hair, browner and scragglier, had never been past my shoulders. I had always kept it short, figuring the ancestors wouldn't be offended by my tampering with a lesser gift. "No," I said. "But you should take a shower. Some of those small bits will probably itch."

"It's already ten o'clock. We should go to sleep soon anyway." Satisfied, she glanced at the mirror in the foyer. "I look like a completely different person," she said. She left to take her shower. I wrapped up her hair in the newspapers and went into the kitchen. I stood next to the sink for a long time before throwing the bundle away.

THE past sees through all attempts at disguise. That night I was awakened by my sister's scream. I gasped and stiffened, grabbing a handful of blanket.

"*Claudia*," Emily cried from the other bed. "Claudia, wake up!"

"What is it?"

"I saw Baba." She hadn't called our father Baba in years. "Over there, by the door. Did you see him?"

"No," I said. "I didn't see anything." My bones felt frozen in place. After a moment I opened my eyes. The full moon shone through the window, bathing our room in silver and shadow. I heard my sister sob and then fall silent. I looked carefully at the door, but I noticed nothing.

Then I understood that his ghost would never visit me. I was, one might say, the lucky daughter. But I lay awake until morning, waiting; part of me is waiting still.

PIPA'S STORY

MY MOTHER WORKED IN CHARMS. SHE could brew a drink to brighten eyes or warm the womb. She knew of a douche that would likely bring a male child, and a potion to chase away unborn children. Except in emergencies, she gathered her own herbs and animal parts. I was not allowed to help.

The villagers said she had learned her craft from a Miao tribeswoman. A group of Miao—strangers from the west—had stayed in our village for a few months, shortly after my father's death. My mother had mixed potions to forget, wandering in the woods to learn where mushrooms grew. My earliest memories are of watching the smoke from her kettle: white smoke, blue, gray, and black smoke.

When I was a child she seemed all-powerful, and although time passed and I grew tall, she continued to loom over me until I thought I would disappear if I could not get away from her shadow. When I was nineteen, I decided to leave the village. For days I watched my mother stir a mixture over the stove-kettle. Finally I gathered the courage to speak.

Hunger

"I will go to Shanghai and work for a family there," I said to her back. "I'll send you an envelope filled with money at New Year."

My mother added a bowl of ice that hissed and crackled against whatever was in the pot. Then she turned to look into me. I forced myself to look back into her black eyes.

"Sit down," she told me, gesturing to the wooden chair by the window.

I sat and watched her strain the cooling potion into a wooden bowl. Then she unbraided my hair and combed it, dipping the comb into the potion. It was a warm evening in early spring. The room glowed white in the light of the half-moon.

"What is the potion?" I asked.

"It is a mixture to make you ready for departure."

I lost a breath. My mother tugged and pulled at me, braiding my hair into one thick plait.

"There are herbs here to protect you against bodily harm from illness, loss of energy, and unclear thinking. There are also herbs that will fix your memory, your past. You will never forget me here, no matter how far away you go."

She wrapped the end of my braid around and around with red thread. "You want to leave," she said. "You have my permission if you make one promise to me."

"I promise," I said. Anything if she would let me go.

She looked out the window to make sure that no one was standing by. "Come here," she said. I followed her to a corner of the room, where it was dark.

Three steps from the corner my mother knelt down and began digging into the dirt with a spoon. She unearthed a small box, muddy but with dull tin showing in patches. We walked to the window, where we could see. My mother opened the box, took something out, and handed it to me.

It was a lump, smaller than the palm of my hand, wrapped in rough cotton.

"Open it," she said.

I unfolded the cloth. Inside glowed a pinkish stone, a craggy piece of our mountain.

"Lao Fu will take you to Shanghai," my mother said. "Find work with a family named Wen. They have a large household and probably many servants. You're still rough, straight from the country, and they may not want to hire you, but I'm sure you can persuade them. Don't tell them that you're from this village, and don't tell them my name."

"Why not?"

"That doesn't concern you. If you don't like working for the Wens, you may leave and go wherever you like, but before you leave, you must do this one thing for me."

"What is it?"

"Find the heart of the house," she said. "It's a huge, modern place. I am sure. Wen will have become involved with western business, and he will have a large western-style house. You'll have to spend some time searching. Let the house seep around you; listen for its rhythm. Before three months are up, find the center and hide this stone there."

"What are you talking about?" I asked rudely. "I never learned anything about houses. You never told me. How would I know?"

My mother didn't scold me but squatted on the floor and looked into the beam of pale moonlight.

"Tell me," she said, "where the heart of our own house is."

I thought for a minute. Then I pointed to the middle of the floor.

"No," she said. "The physical center is not what I mean."

Hunger

I sighed. Our house—a hut, really—was quite small, and as far as I could tell had no other center. We had a table, our beds, two old chairs. The corner shelf held storybooks: *Dream of the Red Chamber* and *Outlaws of the Marsh*, that my mother had been teaching me to read for years. Our house had no male presence, because my father had died before I was born. My mother earned our living. I thought about my mother, her long gray braid hanging down her back, hunched before the stove-kettle full of glowing coals.

"The fire," I said. "The stove is the heart of our house."

My mother nodded. "Good," she said.

At her praise I felt cold and heavy. "What is this about?"

She shook her head. "It's better if you don't know," she said. "It was before you were born. Your deed will be the end of it." She stood up and walked to the window again. "It's something that happened long ago."

I LEFT with the stone sewn into my pocket. I rode in a cart with Lao Fu, my mother's old friend, who was bringing medicine roots to sell around the city. These roots were much like ginseng, and grew wild on our mountain. I watched Lao Fu's thick, arthritic hands on the reins, carelessly guiding his spotted horse. Now and then he flicked a tattered whip. In those days it took weeks to reach Shanghai. Lao Fu didn't usually make such long trips. He was taking me as a favor to my mother, who often rubbed an ointment into his knuckles. We didn't speak for hours, by which time the most familiar mountains had grown pale blue in the distance and we were surrounded by shapes I had seen before only from far away. Then Lao Fu turned an eye to me.

"You're a *nenggan* girl, Pipa," he said in his rusty

voice. "A capable, dutiful girl. Traveling hundreds of miles in order to help your mother."

He smiled, exposing four brown teeth. I glared at the stains on his gray beard and I wished that someone else were driving me, someone I had never met. Even in this remote region the lines of the surrounding hills seemed to shape my mother's face. The stone in my pocket, my secret, weighed so heavily I could hardly sit upright. I wanted to rip it out of my smock and fling it into the next river. She would never know.

But when we reached Shanghai I felt so terrified by my first view of the great port that I held onto the stone like a talisman. I sat close to Lao Fu, dreading our approach to the Wen house, where he would leave me. The city seemed to whirl past. The wide streets were cluttered with travelers—in carts like ours, but also in rickshaws and automobiles. I had never seen either before, nor had I seen the kind of people, foreigners, who rode in them.

In those days foreigners were everywhere: stiff soldiers in uniforms from England and America, businessmen from Russia, hurrying in and out of large, square western buildings. I sat paralyzed, blocking my ears against the roaring, honking automobiles. I turned away from the rickshawmen, their faces drawn, their feet slap-slapping against the pavement. We stopped at an intersection. I saw a man with yellow eyes lurch toward our cart. Lao Fu twitched his whip in that direction. "Opium," he said. "Don't look."

On another corner I spotted a powerfully built Chinese man dressed in western clothes, his short, glossy hair oiled back from his forehead. He was talking to three foreigners, standing as straight as any of them. For a moment he seemed to stare at our cart, at Lao Fu adjusting a strap on the harness. Then he looked away.

As we went on the shops and businesses gave way

to houses: tall brick boxes set back from the road, with no round doorways or Chinese courtyards. Shining black automobiles veered around us. One of them nearly struck the horse. I turned to Lao Fu in alarm, but he merely shook his head and guided our cart closer to the side of the road.

"Lao Fu, where are we?"

"Close."

After one more street he turned right. The horse clip-clopped around a long bend, and suddenly we were twenty yards from an entrance to an immense house built of brick and wood. I saw a woman watching us from a window. Lao Fu stopped the cart.

"Here you are, Pipa. That door is the servants' entrance." I stared at my lap. "*Xialai.* Get down. I'll take your bundle."

I climbed from the cart, my legs stiff, clutching the stone in my pocket. Lao Fu came around the back of the cart holding my blue cotton bundle.

"Go in," he said. I wrinkled my mouth to hold back tears. "You will be all right," he said. "I'll be in the surrounding towns for a few months. I'll come visit you."

We faced each other and bobbed our heads. Lao Fu climbed back onto his cart and picked up the reins. He nodded again before turning away.

I stood watching his cart go back around the bend. I realized that I had said goodbye to the last of the village, and to my mother. After years of avoiding her sight, I had gone to a place where she could not see me. Suddenly I was filled with an emotion so terrible that I turned and vomited at the side of the road.

A VERY pretty girl stood at the servants' door, waiting. She wore black pants and a clean white blouse. From the way her hair was done, I guessed that she had been the one looking out the window.

"Are you all right?" she asked in a low, pleasant voice. Close up, I stood a head taller than she.

"Yes," I said. I clutched my bundle. "I want to work here."

Her glance darted over my rough cotton clothes. "Come in," she said. "Clean up inside. You should bathe, and change. Then I'll introduce you to the housekeeper."

I walked into the great house and smelled the warm, rich odor of food and spices. We stood in a square room lined with wood. A door to my right opened into a hallway. I could see at the end a room where a number of people were chopping vegetables.

"Come here quickly," whispered the girl, darting toward another doorway. She led me to a very white, shining room with a long white basin on four feet. I had never seen a bathtub before, and I stopped to stare. The girl, who said her name was Meilan, turned two silver fixtures at one end of the tub, and steaming water poured out of a pipe. She held a huge towel in front of me so that I wouldn't be embarrassed while she stayed in the room.

I took off my dirty traveling clothes and stepped into the tub. The warm water rushed around my body, erasing the village dirt. I unbraided my hair, and my mother's spells were washed away in a swirl of steam. I felt myself changing, like a tadpole, and I looked at my hands and limbs as if they were new.

Behind her towel Meilan chattered away.

"Of course they'll hire you; the family just moved into this new residence, and they need servants. They hired me only three months ago. I'll have you fixed up so that no one will think twice."

"Why did you come to work here?" I asked.

"I'm from Beijing. My mother died giving birth to me, and my father was in the Kuomindang Army. He died last year in the fighting. I am an orphan. I had to find work. This is a good place. The master is rich and good-looking. Supervision is not very strict."

After a minute I asked, "Fighting? What fighting?"

"You really are from far away! There's been terrible fighting, not in Shanghai, but maybe soon!" Her voice dropped, and I had to lean close to the towel in order to hear.

"I don't know anything about these events," I said. "Our village is so remote, even the Japanese ignored it."

When I was finished, she found a pair of black trousers and a white shirt that were both a little too small for me. "We'll get some others after you've started," she said. "I'll steal them from the closet."

"Thank you for helping me," I said.

Meilan smiled. "This is nothing," she answered. "There is plenty here; why not share it? And besides, you look like a nice person." She picked up my old blue cotton smock. "Do you want this saved?"

I thought of the stone sewn into the pocket. "No," I said.

WEN lived on one of the most stylish new streets in Shanghai. For weeks I marveled at his house; I had never even dreamed of anything like it. The rooms were broad and tall, with glossy, patterned wooden floors built by English carpenters and covered with flowered Persian carpets. English curtains draped down by long windows, deep red velvet curtains with gold-colored tasseled cords. Everything in that house was new, from the mysterious electric lights to the great wooden tubs in the kitchen, filled with live clams in salt water in case one of the family should have a craving for them.

The housekeeper, Lu Taitai, was an immense older woman whose face lay as still as a mud bog. When she was very angry, she would slowly lift one fat finger into the air. I lived in terror of her. I was the newest of thirty servants, so unskilled that at first I worked in the servants' quarters, which, as Meilan pointed out, had to be kept clean along with the rest of the house. Meilan's swift hands and pretty face had earned her a job on the third floor, where the family lived. I imagined that the upstairs must be a magical place.

"Can you show me the upper floors?" I asked her once, as we ate dinner at one end of the long servants' table.

She looked right and left before answering. "We have to watch out for Lu Taitai," she said. "And it's harder to get away with things upstairs. The women have sharp eyes. If I have a chance, I'll take you."

"What women?" I asked. "The servant women?"

Meilan put down her chopsticks. "Pipa," she said, "the master has four wives." She smiled. "Stop blushing, and keep eating."

I looked at the table. We ate what Wen and his family left. The night before, they had feasted on duck done ten ways, and there was a pile of crackling duck skins, which I had discovered I particularly liked. There were also jelled duck eggs, pigeon eggs in sauce, shrimps with chicken and peas, chicken and scallops with ginger, scallops in sauce, salted prawns, spicy prawns, late oysters, early asparagus, several other vegetable dishes, and a great fish that lay on its side, barely touched. I thought that if a man was wealthy enough to serve four dishes for each member of the family, then perhaps four wives was to be expected.

HUNGER

A FEW weeks later Lu Taitai was suddenly called away to her home province.

"Good," Meilan said. By flirting with the second housekeeper, she arranged for me to bring tea to the master upstairs in his library, during a meeting with some of his western associates.

"If it weren't for you, I would be lost," I said when I thanked her. "I've been here for a month and I've never seen him."

"Well," she said, "he's very good-looking. I can see why the women fall for him: rich, handsome, and powerful! But even so, I don't think I'd want to be the object of his attention. I have a feeling he's not very kind—that he simply doesn't take kindness, or certain human feelings, into account. Of course, he seldom looks at people like you and me. We can only watch. But if that's what you want, my dear friend Pipa, you shall have it." And she made me practice several times with the bamboo tea tray.

On the day of the meeting, we waited to hear the men's heavy shoes start up the staircase. "Go up now," Meilan said. She fixed some of the coarse hair that had escaped from my pinned-up braid. The cook's assistant stared with grim disapproval while I balanced the tray.

For the first time I climbed the polished staircase.

The second floor was quiet. The carpet melted under my feet. Meilan had instructed me: "Turn left at the top, go down two doors, and you've reached the library." The heavy, unfamiliar tray hindered my progress; delicate teacups slid on their bits of lace. I reached the library door, braced the tray as securely as possible against my hip, and knocked.

"Come in," said a resonant male voice.

I looked at the big china knob. How could I possibly

turn it? I moved to brace my feet and felt the smooth wood tray slide against my blouse.

Suddenly the door opened and a man stood over me, holding a book in one hand. For a moment I forgot my manners and stared. I had seen him before: the arrogant man whom I had noticed while riding with Lao Fu on my first day in Shanghai. Now he stood and looked at my face, my blouse, my hands holding the tray. I felt as if a piece of burning ash had been put down my back. I gasped; the tray tilted in my hands. The house with its soft rugs fought against me, making me lose my balance. Hot tea spilled on the master's arm and over the book he carried.

"*Duibuqi,*" I gasped, hastily putting down the ruined tray. I grabbed an embroidered linen napkin and reached to dry his arm.

"I'm fine," he said. "Dry this." He handed me the book, and even in my horror it occurred to me that this man must have strength not to so much as flinch at the boiling water. I waited for him to scold me, or even strike me, but he did not move.

"*Duibuqi,*" I repeated, and indeed at that moment I did not think I could ever look him in the face again. I wiped the pages. "*Xianggang Falu,*" I read aloud. Why was he studying Hong Kong laws?

"You can read," he said.

"My mother taught me," I blurted out.

"Then you'll still be of some use to us," he said. "It's obvious you're not a good maid. Come in."

I tiptoed into the room. Opposite me stood three crowded bookshelves. The foreigners sat at the end, before the fireplace.

"You're tall," said Wen. "You can read. Find the books I want and bring them over. Find me the volume about transportation on the Yangtze and the Grand Canal."

I turned to the shelves, my hands sweating. Wen went back to the fireplace.

"If you want factual proof, I'll give it to you," I heard him say to the foreigners. "But I guarantee, they'll wait. They've won too many battles too quickly. They need to regroup. It will be months before they reach Shanghai, maybe a year. You needn't worry."

Someone coughed. "Oh, certainly, certainly." This man spoke Chinese with difficulty. "It's just that we have received some—reports from further north. Of course," he continued, searching for the words, "we're not worried about them. The Kuomindang troops have regrouped themselves to defend our side of the Yangtze.... We are just—making sure that we understand the situation."

"Those who flee are fools," Wen said. "I tell you, it's not time to leave yet. They would never touch a foreigner. Remember, the longer you stay, the more you'll make."

"And you as well," said one of the men.

"You can believe me." Wen's voice grew hard. "I know what Mao will do. I'm one of them. I was born a peasant, you know."

In the bottom right corner of the shelf I spotted a blue volume on waterways, which I pulled and brought to Wen. I watched as he studied the book, the firelight flickering on his face, and I could sense his force, his intelligence and cunning.

"Ha!" he said, pointing to a line of characters. "You see, I was correct." He showed the book to one of the western gentlemen, who squinted, nervously stroking his blond beard.

"What does it say, Stanton?" one of them asked.

"Ah, yes! Mr. Wen is correct," Stanton said. I wondered if he could read characters well enough to know what he was talking about.

"Now," Wen said, "about those collections. I'll have the first half to you by Monday next week." He turned to me. "You can go now," he said. "I'll call you the next time there is a meeting."

As I left the library, I saw the tea tray sitting in the hallway. I bent down to pick it up.

"What are you doing?" asked a musical, imperious voice.

I straightened. I had not heard her walk across the carpet. She was tiny, beautiful, with large eyes and a curved lower lip like an orange slice. She wore a *qipao* of shimmering sea-green silk.

"I came with the tea," I tried to explain. "I was helping in the library."

"*Helping*," she said. Her eyes flickered up and down my body.

"Getting books."

Her lower lip swelled with dissatisfaction. She walked past me to the library door. "Are they still inside?"

I nodded.

She lifted her chin. "Hmph!" she said. "Get back downstairs."

I picked up the tray and hurried away, cold tea splashing on the carpet.

Downstairs, Meilan waited for me.

"I was worried!" she cried. But when I explained what had happened, she smiled and patted my arm. "Now you've earned your job in the house. No more rag-pushing for you!" Her eyes sparkled.

"YOUR mother will want to know how you are doing," Lao Fu said.

I didn't answer. Lao Fu guided his horse past two arguing street peddlers. He had returned to the city and come by to take me on a ride. I felt ashamed that the others would see me with him, with his patched clothes and shabby cart. But it was a beautiful day in May. The fresh warm air reminded me how seldom I had a chance to go outside, now that I was working at the Wen house.

"Before we left, she asked me to check on you," Lao Fu said, "and to ask you if you kept your promise."

"Why is everything so crowded?" I asked, changing the subject. Even on the quieter streets we could not drive in a straight line.

"In the past few months more and more people north of us have fled the Red Army, seeking safety."

"Where is the Army now?"

"Since the end of the year it has been waiting north of the Yangtze River."

I remembered the conversation in the library. "What will happen when it moves south again?"

Lao Fu looked at me, and I saw his cloudy cataracts. "Things will change."

"How will they change?"

"Ah," he said. "Who knows? These days I demand only coppers in payment. The Kuomindang is crumbling. Why won't you answer your mother's question?"

"I don't have time to think about her anymore," I said.

Lao Fu ignored me. "Look over there," he said. "A decent noodle house, and not too busy. Let's have lunch."

After we had taken care of the cart and horse, we stood for a minute outside the noodle shop, watching the people on the street. A thin man carrying a large wicker basket shuffled close to us. "*Zhuan qian, zhuan qian,*" he repeated under his breath. Lao Fu nodded and handed him a few coppers. The man opened his basket and counted out sixteen bundles of paper money. They nodded at each other, and we entered the dark, noisy noodle shop.

"You see?" Lao Fu said as we sat down at a corner table. "By the time we leave, those coppers will be worth sixteen and a half bundles of paper money."

I felt as if he were saying these things to make a point against me. Stubbornly I folded my hands in my lap.

"What will happen when the Communist Army reaches this city?" Lao Fu lit his long pipe. "They'll go after people like your master, rich people who flourished under the Kuomindang by working with foreign capitalists. There's a word for your master, Pipa. He's an *ermaozi*, a comprador."

"He's a peasant," I said. "He's a former peasant who used his wits to make a fortune for himself, to move away from his village."

"Ha," Lao Fu said. He fitted his pipe between his four stubby teeth. "You're a young girl, Pipa. You're young, and the world is a strange place."

I scowled and took a sip of the tea that a greasy-haired, smudge-faced woman had flung on the table.

"What difference do his origins make to you?" I asked. "You're here with a message from my mother. You don't know Master Wen or anything about him."

"But I do know him," Lao Fu said. "I used to know him well."

I stared at my wavering saucer of tea.

"When he was a young man in the village, we used to call him Xiao Niu, Little Bull. He was once a friend of your father's."

There was a terrible pounding in my ears. Lao Fu's rusty voice sounded like a shout. I waited for him to stop, but he continued. "Some people forget their histories, but they don't realize that others remember," he said. "Not everyone forgets the wrongs they've suffered."

He raised the saucer to his mouth. His loud slurp brought me back to my senses.

"What do you mean?" I forced out the words.

"Ah. Well, this is an old story. Something that happened before you were born. It is, shall I say, a village secret."

"There aren't any secrets in the village."

"Well, it's possible. There were only four of us who knew. One died, one has forgotten, and two of us have chosen not to tell. That is, until now."

At that moment the woman brought us two broad, steaming bowls of noodle soup. Lao Fu nodded. "Good. Eat."

I took a spoonful of soup, waiting. The food and even the serving utensils were so much coarser than what I had grown used to.

Lao Fu began. "Your father and mother were the two village orphans. No one arranged their marriage. When they wed, it was a love match."

He took a mouthful of noodles and went on. My father, he said, was gentle and kind. He had spent years learning to read in his spare time; he sat and daydreamed over his meals. My mother was clever, forceful. She never rested. And she had an astounding talent that everyone in the village knew about. If an object was lost, my mother could almost always find it. On the mountains she understood the natural order and discovered more medicine roots than anyone else. It was she who suggested that she and my father supplement their income by collecting medicine roots. Xiao Niu and Lao Fu agreed to help them.

"There was one problem," Lao Fu said. "Perhaps because she was so sure of herself, your mother underestimated Xiao Niu. He was a ruthless, ambitious boy who wanted to be the best at everything. And the more he saw of your mother, the more he wanted her as well. He desired her. He wanted to stop her constant thinking and doing; he wanted her to think and do only for him.

"Your mother was not beautiful, but she had so much

vitality that she was impossible to ignore. She knew that Xiao Niu wanted her, but she thought she could control him. This goaded Xiao Niu until he couldn't bear it."

One cloudy fall day the four of them had gone to dig for medicine roots. For part of the day they worked together. All morning Xiao Niu watched my mother out of the corner of his eye. After lunch my mother suggested that they split up and search on different parts of the mountain. And Xiao Niu suggested he and my father go off together.

That afternoon the fog grew so thick that my mother and Lao Fu, working close together, could hardly see each other. It was very quiet. The path became almost impossible to find; trees and stones looked like people and animals. If it hadn't been for my mother, Lao Fu said, they might not have found the pathway down the mountain, back to the village.

When they reached the village, my mother waited for Xiao Niu and my father to return. She built a fire, cooked the evening meal. But the other two did not come back. She began to worry. Finally, after the gray fog had turned dark, Xiao Niu stopped by our hut.

"Where's Dangbei?" he asked.

"What do you mean?" my mother said. "I thought he was with you."

"He left early," Xiao Niu told her. "He decided to go back to the village."

All that night my mother waited, but my father did not come home.

The next day my mother went out on the mountain, in the fog, searching for him. She looked and looked, but she could not find him. Finally some men from the village had to force her to stay inside—she was pregnant, after all. Then winter set in.

"All winter, your mother mourned," Lao Fu said.

Hunger

"She would only speak to me and Xiao Niu. Xiao Niu asked her to marry him, but she refused to discuss anything until your father's body was discovered. That spring, right before you were born, the villagers found him at the bottom of a ravine, lying on a bed of pinkish stones. After the birth your mother insisted on going up on the mountain to look upon the spot where they had found his body.

"Now here is the secret," Lao Fu said. "Your mother told only me. After seeing the site where your father's body was discovered, she felt certain that he had not gotten there on his own. If the two of them had gone to dig in the place Xiao Niu had described, your father would not have died where his body was found."

"How did she know?" I asked. "On foggy days in our mountains, a person could wander anywhere."

"I asked her. 'I know Dangbei,' she said. 'He would never have gotten lost there,' she said. And I believed her. She knew the mountains. I felt foolish and angry. So much had been going on right under my nose, and I had not understood."

He looked at me. I ignored him, studying my soup. "I was younger those days, and I hated being wrong about things," he said.

"That summer Xiao Niu again asked her to marry him. She accused him of killing Dangbei, and Xiao Niu left the village. He disappeared for years, and when we heard about him next, he had taken the name of Wen."

After this my mother had begun to brood before the stove, to speak to Miao travelers and learn their arts. She was unable to forget what had been lost.

"Now," Lao Fu said when the story was finished and our bowls were empty, "when I return to the village, your mother will ask me if you have kept your promise to her."

I looked at him. He leaned toward me; a noodle hung

from his beard. I felt my eyes grow hot with confusion and anger. Despite my own intentions, my loyalties had changed. He had cast her shadow over me again, and I could not forgive him.

"Leave me alone!" I said. "You tell my mother that I will not keep my promise to her. None of this has anything to do with me. I'm far away, and she can't reach me. She can't make me do what I don't want to do. Besides, it's impossible now."

Lao Fu's wrinkled lids lowered. He nodded. "You do what you must do. I'll be in the city another week—"

"Don't visit me anymore," I said.

BACK at Wen's house the servants were getting ready for an important business dinner. I looked for Meilan. I wanted to talk to her, but the second housekeeper gave me a pile of rags and some scented oil, and put me to work on the yards of rich wood panelling in the sitting room and dining room.

As I wiped and polished, certain thoughts traced themselves over and over in my mind. The scented oil filled my nostrils, reminding me of my mother's potions. I remembered her sorting out bundles of herbs on our wooden table, her frown deepening in the firelight. She had loved my father, whom I had never met. For years I had secretly believed that the purpose of her herbs, her potions, and her utterances, was not to help the others but to keep me near her. But now it seemed that even my flight from her fit into some incomprehensible design. I began to see that Lao Fu was right. I was young; the world was a mystery.

I finished the woodwork and walked into the hall. And for the first time I noticed something odd about Wen's house. I saw the great house, with its women and servants, as a testimony to the unquenchable desire of its master, desire that destroyed all obstacles and then discarded them. The house seemed raw and unexplained, as if it were hiding its origin. The rooms were big and empty: too clean, too new, too cold. I looked down the hall at the dozen servants cleaning and sweeping as if there were more than dirt to get rid of.

As I entered the dining room, one of the rags dropped out of my hands and fell to the wooden floor with a small thud. I knelt down to pick it up, but then I stopped, crouching, and stared at the rough blue cotton fabric.

Snatching the rag, I sprang up and ran toward the staircase. I had to find Meilan, my friend, and tell her what had happened. I needed to hear what she would say. I had to see her. I pounded up the stairs, past the second floor, and up to the family quarters.

The upstairs was lit by the fading light from a few windows. I had never been up so high before, but I remembered the stories from the servants' table: the four wives each in a suite of rooms, and at one end the master's room, near a separate staircase to the outside door, so he could get away. The doors were closed. Sweet scents of soap and perfume filled the air. They must all be getting ready for dinner. I would never find Meilan.

I heard a doorknob turn, then another door open and shut. I saw two doors at the north end, and one was ajar. I hurried toward it and ran straight into Meilan coming out. When I saw her face, I forgot to think for a moment.

"What's wrong?" I cried.

Meilan buried her face in her hands. "Oh!" she sobbed. "It's terrible—I have to get away from here! I can't work here any more."

"What happened?" I asked. She clutched herself around the waist and ran down the hall. I followed her down the two flights of stairs, rushing past a few surprised-looking servants. "Meilan," I begged, "let me help you!"

She ran into the room we shared with some other servants.

"Please let me help you," I said. "You're always so kind to me."

"Do you have a clean shirt?" she whimpered, her arms still crossed. "Mine are in the wash."

"It'll be too big," I said. But I handed her one. She reached for it, and I saw the rip in the one that she had on. She took off her torn shirt. I saw four blue bruises, in the shape of fingerprints, on her arm. More bruises were on her chest.

Then I knew what I had to do. I found a pair of scissors and cut the stone from the rag I still held in my hand. I went back up the stairs, past the second floor and the library, up to the third floor. The door to the master's room was still ajar. The shades were closed, but I made out a huge square shape in the semi-darkness. I walked to the great canopied bed, and I hid the stone inside it.

When I came back downstairs, Meilan and her things were gone.

LATE that night I was asked to work in the library. My eyes smarting with weariness, I searched the tall bookcases in the flickering light from the fireplace.

"You're making a mistake," I heard him say. "They won't harm you or your business. You'd be better off staying in China and keeping what you have. There's no telling what will happen if you run off and leave everything."

The men by the fire said nothing.

"They would never touch you," he said.

Hunger

After a minute, one of the foreigners spoke. "What will happen to you, Wen? Where are you burying your money? How much of it have you sent abroad?"

"I told you," Wen said. "How could they betray one of their own kind? They won't get me."

Finally I found the book he wanted, and he dismissed me for the evening. The room was utterly silent as I left.

I went downstairs, put on my nightclothes, and lay in bed.

When I shut my eyes, I found that I had grown as light as a straw. I floated high on the wind over Wen's great house and back to where I had come from. I soared over the rich green Yangtze Delta, with its fishermen and rice paddies, following the broad river as it narrowed into rushing rapids, and then continuing westward toward the mountains of my village. Evening fell; the stars wheeled over my head. When I landed, the air smelled of thawed earth and sweet plum blossoms. I walked quietly down the dark road, past the well, and to the corner where my mother's hut stood, slightly sagging.

I looked through the window. Her face was deeply grooved, bloodless with concentration. She had unbraided her long gray hair. She sat cross-legged in the firelight in front of a group of small paper figures. Her voice rattled into the air, making an incantation. She swayed, muttering low deep sounds under her breath, an endless curse word. I looked at the firepot; coals glowed through the slits in its iron sides. I watched through the window until my vision faded into smoke.

Sometime after midnight I was awakened by the sound of gunfire. It was May 12, and the Communist Army had reached the outskirts of Shanghai.

CONSIDERING the events that have since taken place in China and the world, my own story is small and not very interesting. But it is mine. Like ginseng roots, our buried pasts have different shapes. I never saw my mother again. After Lao Fu rescued me from Wen's house, I fled to Taiwan. A year later I met up with a man from our village who told me what had happened there: the Communists had reached the village a few months after the fall of Shanghai, and they had executed my mother as a witch.

In Taiwan, I worked at a library. Now I shelve books in the Chinese collection at an American university. I have a husband and two children who both attended college. We own our own small house. I don't keep the house too clean, and I tried not to frighten my daughters the way my mother frightened me. But there are things I can't forget, and things my family knows they should never do. They do not light fires in the fireplace, not even if I won't be home for hours. For the smell of smoke, the faintest trace, reminds me of my mother.

I see her brooding over her past and I remember that it's not wise to look back too long and deep at what has gone. It is not wise to think of Shanghai, the broad houses now shabby and sectioned off for twenty families. Or to dwell too long on my friend Meilan and her generosity. Or to remember the fire that the Communists started when they reached our section of the city.

The flames leaped through the house, feeding themselves along the expensive wood paneling, ruffling the curtains, exploding the leaded-glass windows. I stood outside with the other servants and watched the sparks and ashes fly up into the night. We looked on as four soldiers led our master out onto the lawn. The soldiers wore red stars on their caps. They struck the back of his knees to make him kneel to them. He knelt with his head high and with anger burning in his face. One of them raised a long machete, twirling the knife so the blunt side came down on the back of his neck to make him fall forward. There was a moment when we were silent; only flames moved. Then the soldier raised his arm again, and the sharp blade sliced all our lives in two.

ACKNOWLEDGMENTS

Many thanks to James A. Michener and the Copernicus Society of America, the Henfield Foundation, the Truman Capote Literary Trust, the University of Iowa Writers' Workshop, and the Stanford Creative Writing Program for their generous support during the writing of this book.

I would also like to thank Sarah Chalfant, my agent, and Jill Bialosky, my editor at W. W. Norton, for their belief in me and their hard work on my behalf.

I am deeply grateful to all of my teachers, especially Frank Conroy, Margot Livesey, James Alan McPherson, Marilynne Robinson, and Elizabeth Tallent. Many thanks also to John L'Heureux, who gave wise counsel above and beyond the call of duty.

The following people have inspired me through their advice and living example: Eavan Boland, Connie Brothers, Gish Jen, Deborah Kwan, D. R. MacDonald, Nancy Packer, Gay Pierce, Susan Power, Lois Rosenthal, and Tobias Wolff. Thanks also to Nell Bernstein and the writers at Pacific News Service.

I am indebted to these friends for their insightful assistance with the manuscript: Geoffrey Becker, Helen Cho, Eileen Chow, Nan Cohen, Alyssa Haywoode, V. Diane

WoodBrown, Deborah Yaffe, and, for reading my work more often than anyone else, Ray Isle. To the following friends, also, I give my deepest thanks for their kindness, wit, and listening skills that have kept me going: Eileen Bartos, Andrea Bewick, Craig Collins, Scott Johnston, and especially Elizabeth Rourke.

Finally, I would like to thank my wise and inspiring parents, Helen Chung-Hung Chang and Nai Lin Chang, and my sisters, who can do anything: Ling Chang, Tina Chang, and Tai Chang Terry.

LAN SAMANTHA CHANG was born and raised in Appleton, Wisconsin. A graduate of Yale University and the University of Iowa, she is the recipient of a National Endowment for the Arts grant, a Wallace Stegner Fellowship from Stanford University, and a Guggenheim Fellowship. *Hunger* won a California Book Award and was a finalist for the *Los Angeles Times* Art Seidenbaum Award. Chang is also the author of the novels *Inheritance* (2004), which won the PEN Open Book Award, and *All Is Forgotten, Nothing Is Lost* (2010). Her novel *The Family Chao* (2022) won an Anisfield-Wolf Book Award for Fiction. Chang lives with her husband and daughter in Iowa City, Iowa, where she is director of the Iowa Writers' Workshop.

HUNGER

Lan Samantha Chang

DISCUSSION QUESTIONS

1. How does the title novella set the stage for the stories that follow? What themes were you able to trace throughout the book, and how were they adapted or expanded so that no two scenes or situations, however similar, seemed repetitive?

2. In several of these stories, and especially in "The Unforgetting," the acts of remembering and forgetting bring about real, tangible change—they're not just mental exercises. How do Chang's characters act out these processes, and why?

3. In "Hunger," Min writes, "I began to understand that to love another was to be a custodian of that person's decline" (p. 62). How and why do Min and other characters stick out difficult relationships? How does one partner's decline, either physical or emotional, affect the other?

4. In the stories, especially those in which immigrant parents raise their children to speak English, language plays an important role. How does it divide people? When does it bring them together? What forms of expression take over when a parent, for example, doesn't speak his/her child's strongest language?

5. In "Hunger," Min wants to tell her daughter that "when you stay in one place long enough, it becomes a part of you whether you want it to or not" (p. 81). Can the immigrants in these stories adapt to new homelands while remaining a part of where they're from? How is this straddling of two worlds both advantageous and devastating?

6. What do the parents in these stories have in common? How do different parents balance the need for leniency and discipline?

7. Can you draw any parallels between Anna from "Hunger" and Charles from "The Unforgetting," or do they seem too dissimilar?

8. Ghosts play a large role in several of Chang's stories, with the dead inhabiting the world of the living. Comparing the ghosts of "Hunger" and "The Eve of the Spirit Festival" to the daughter "seduced by a water ghost" (p. 125) in "Water Names," can you hazard any guesses as to why Chang uses ghosts as characters?

9. How do the children in "Hunger" both seek and deny their parents' approval? Why is there often a "good daughter" and a "bad daughter," and are these roles fixed?

10. Children including Anna, Ruth, Caroline, and Charles exhibit extraordinary talents—for mathematics, music, the study of history, etc. How are their abilities both a burden and an escape? How do these talents allow them to become independent individuals?

11. Both "Water Names" and "Pipa's Story" have mystical elements that distinguish them from the grittier, more mundane realities of the other stories. How does Chang evoke this atmosphere of magic, of uniqueness?

12. What role does China play for the characters? How is it possible that one person might perceive it paradoxically as both familiar and foreign, appealing and yet something to be forgotten?

13. In "San," Caroline describes, "The charm of Brooklyn, this wide shabby street bustling with immigrants like ourselves, was enough to make [my father] feel lucky" (p. 136). How is New York perceived by the Chinese who move there? Do they see it and America as a "melting pot" for them?

14. Chang's characters often point out the physical and emotional similarities between parents and their children. How do some of these children "become their parents"? Can inheritance and environment trump personal desire, or is there something else about the children that keeps them from turning out differently?

15. Chang pits rational thinking against superstition and religious ritual. Give some examples of moments in which faith wins out over the rational, and others in which rational thinking defeats superstition. Do you think Chang is more comfortable with faith or rationality?